THE HEIRESS'S BABY

LILIAN DARCY

D0003849

SPECIAL EDITION®

Published by Silhouette Books

America's Publisher of Contemporary Romance

If you purchased this book without a cover you should be aware that this book is stolen property. It was reported as "unsold and destroyed" to the publisher, and neither the author nor the publisher has received any payment for this "stripped book."

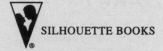

SILHOUETTE BOOKS

ISBN-13: 978-0-373-65545-8

THE HEIRESS'S BABY

Recycling programs for this product may not exist in your area.

Copyright © 2010 by Lilian Darcy

All rights reserved. Except for use in any review, the reproduction or utilization of this work in whole or in part in any form by any electronic, mechanical or other means, now known or hereafter invented, including xerography, photocopying and recording, or in any information storage or retrieval system, is forbidden without the written permission of the editorial office, Silhouette Books, 233 Broadway, New York, NY 10279 U.S.A.

This is a work of fiction. Names, characters, places and incidents are either the product of the author's imagination or are used fictitiously, and any resemblance to actual persons, living or dead, business establishments, events or locales is entirely coincidental.

This edition published by arrangement with Harlequin Books S.A.

For questions and comments about the quality of this book please contact us at Customer_eCare@Harlequin.ca.

® and TM are trademarks of Harlequin Books S.A., used under license. Trademarks indicated with ® are registered in the United States Patent and Trademark Office, the Canadian Trade Marks Office and in other countries.

Visit Silhouette Books at www.eHarlequin.com

Printed in U.S.A.

LILIAN DARCY

has written nearly eighty books for Silhouette Romance, Silhouette Special Edition and Harlequin Medical Romance (Prescription Romance). Happily married, with four active children and a very patient cat, she enjoys keeping busy and could probably fill several more lifetimes with the things she likes to do—including cooking, gardening, quilting, drawing and traveling. She currently lives in Australia but travels to the United States as often as possible to visit family. Lilian loves to hear from readers. You can write to her at P.O. Box 532, Jamison P.O., Macquarie ACT 2614, Australia, or e-mail her at: lilian@liliandarcy.com.

Chapter One

August, San Diego

Lannie was still in the bathroom.

Nate had spent the past half hour in the hotel bar downstairs having coffee with his sister Krystal, a rendezvous that she had called "putting our heads together and coming up with a strategy" and he'd mentally renamed "hitting up her big brother for money." Lannie had been in the bathroom when he left their luxurious room, and she was still in there now.

Or was she?

It was very quiet in there. The door was closed. No sound of shower water running, no whine from a blow dryer, or the little chinking sounds of make-up items being placed on a marble surface. He listened, feeling as if he was invading her privacy, feeling his stress levels rise. Thanks to the latest drama with his family, those levels had been high to begin with.

His mind circled pointlessly as he attempted to solve his

sister's problems. He'd written her a check for the money she wanted, discharging her latest debt and more, but would it really help? What could he do that might have a snowball's chance of yielding a more long-term benefit?

And as for his mother...

It wasn't something he could deal with this minute, he told himself. Stick with what was really important.

Was Lannie okay?

Was she in there?

Or had she bailed on him, ordered a car for the airport and taken the next flight out of San Diego, the way he'd half-expected her to ever since they'd arrived on Thursday? He'd seen her checking airline schedules on her phone last night.

He pivoted toward the mirror-fronted closets and wrenched open the doors, seriously expecting a gaping void instead of the six or seven gorgeous outfits that had been hanging there half an hour ago. He deserved it, really. He could have made the past few days easier for her, if he'd tried. He could have kept her away from Friday's dinner, refused to let her help with everything on Saturday. He could have refused the coffee with Krystal, told his sister to deal with her own problems— or simply cut to the chase and written her the check while standing in the hotel lobby.

In the closet he saw the flashes of bright color. Gold, red, sepia, green... Lannie's outfits were still there, neatly hung above a line of matching shoes.

His heartbeat slowed again and the blood stopped beating in his ears. For a long moment, relief made him light-headed.

She hadn't left.

She was still here.

He caught sight of his reflection in the mirror and saw the tension in his tightly held fists, his dark hair rumpled and overdue for a cut, the shirt tail that had come untucked.

Then he heard the sound of the faucets running in the bathroom basin and reverted to his original, and almost as stressful, question. So if Lannie hadn't bailed out of San Diego—out of Nate's life—why had she been in the bathroom for so long? Was she okay?

"Lannie?" he finally called out.

"Yup, I'm here." Her voice sounded strange.

"Are you okay?" It seemed lame to him after he'd been asking it in his head for the past five minutes—not sufficiently concerned, or maybe…new thought…not sufficiently confrontational. He knew they were on a knife edge. They both knew it. There'd been episodes of talking about it, circling around a couple of heavyweight issues, like boxers circling in the ring without throwing a punch. Nothing was resolved. Nothing was even fully *said,* out in the open.

They both just knew.

"I'm…yeah…sort of okay," she answered.

"Sort of?"

"Give me another minute."

More sounds of running water, and a high-pitched whine he recognized as her electric toothbrush, less strident than the blow-dryer. Finally she emerged.

And she wasn't okay.

Even without her pale skin, hair roughly knotted at the back, and water splodges down the front of her top, he'd have known she wasn't okay. The look in her eyes, the tightness around her mouth, the daunted, hunted quality in the way she held her body—all of it so different from how he normally saw her, so bright and beautiful and confident and carelessly—sometimes defiantly—strong. "How was your coffee with Krystal?" she asked.

"Fine. It was fine. The usual. But—"

"Were you right about what she wanted? You were. I can see. What did you—?"

"I don't want to talk about my sister right now. What's the matter? You look—"

"Just give me another moment."

"Tell me," he said.

"I will. I will." She sat on the bed, as if gathering her strength, or sorting through her mind for the right words.

He was torn between wanting her to just say it, cut and dried, to put them both out of their misery, and wanting to put his arms around her, pull that messy twist out of her hair and bury his face in it, breathe it in and kiss her and tell her she didn't need to say it, not yet, not if she didn't want to, not for hours if she didn't want to. To tell her that whatever it was, it would be okay in the long run because he was here, and they were so strong together. They'd work it out. He always managed to work things out. He always stepped up to the plate.

But would she want to hear all that? He didn't think she would.

Instead, he compromised. Sat beside her and took her hand, brushed the skin over her knuckles softly with his thumb. "No hurry, Lannie." Her skin was so soft. He wanted to lift her hand to his face and breathe in the powdery scent of her moisturizer.

He wanted, as always, to take her to bed.

But her thoughts were a thousand miles from anything like that. She seemed to wish that her body was a thousand miles away, also. A thousand miles from him. A thousand miles from whatever had happened in the bathroom and was still haunting her.

She took a big, wobbly breath, pressed her palms against her cheeks as if to cool her heated skin, raked her perfect teeth over her lower lip. "I don't want you to think I've been—that I've been holding this to myself without even hinting. I mean, it didn't add up until just now, when I got sick in there. The various— You know, we've been— The signs, and what they might mean. I didn't put it all together. But now... I'm scared! This is huge! I didn't expect it. I'm not ready. I haven't had time to think. And this trip has been challenging enough. I'm so scared!"

Oh hell...*hell!*

"Just damn well say it, Lannie."

"Okay. Yes." Another breath. She looked at him with burning blue eyes. "I think I must be pregnant, Nate. In fact, I'm almost sure."

Of course. In the space of three seconds, give or take, it went from being the farthest thing from his mind to the most obvious thing in the world.

Of course.

Pregnant.

Life was like that, wasn't it? His mother and sister could both have told him that.

And he knew exactly what must be going on in Lannie's head, exactly what her instincts and her previous track record would tell her to do. She'd always pulled the strategy off so well, in the past.

It had worked for her.

It had helped her survive everything from her parents' conservative and stereotypical expectations to machine-gun toting brigands in a mountain wilderness.

He shouldn't have said it out loud, and it sure as heck shouldn't have been the *first* thing he said, but, hell, this had been a rough few days, and it was one of the big issues they'd been circling around—maybe even *the* issue, as far as he was concerned.

So he opened his mouth and the words just fell out. "Pregnant. And I guess you've already worked out, haven't you, before you even shared the news with me, exactly how you're going to bail?"

Chapter Two

June, Upstate New York

Atlanta Sheridan was not your stereotypical hotel heiress.

Or so Nathan had been told.

Right at this moment, though, she sure looked it. He watched her strutting across the airport tarmac toward him. Her highlighted blonde hair shone in the sunshine of early June and swung in the breeze. It looked as clean and bouncy as if she'd had it styled and cut mid-flight. Her smoothly tanned legs tapered down to shoes with straps the width of dental floss and heels like eight-inch nails. Her sunglasses said, "Look at me!" while supposedly disguising her face, and her outfit screamed a four-figure price tag.

You won't last a month, honey, Nate thought with cynical satisfaction. He liked strong, interesting women, not bimbos. Over the years his serious dates had included an Olympic ski racer, a wildlife photographer, and a professor of forest

ecology, and that was the kind of female company he preferred, both in his personal life and on the job.

A woman like this, on the other hand...

The airport in upstate New York was tiny. Here she was,
coming through the glass door into a building you couldn't
really class as a terminal. More like a prefabricated shed,
about the size of a grade-school classroom with a couple of
offices opening off it, and vending machines covering any
requirement for food and drink.

He stepped forward to greet her. "Ms. Sheridan..."

"Yes, hi, how are you?" She beamed at him, pushed the
sunglasses up on top of her head, then reached out to shake
his hand. Her French manicured nails gleamed as her fingers
slipped against his. Her top lip had a little dent in it, which
meant that even when she closed her mouth her lips looked
as if they were about to part.

Suddenly, he found himself almost stammering. "Good.
I'm great," he said. His wits had to grope for solid ground.
"Nathan Ridgeway. Nate."

She had amazing eyes, as blue as summer water, and an
electric handshake, cool and firm and filled with a kind of
energy he felt but couldn't analyze. Not right now.

Something had happened.

A mix of slamming desire had rushed through him, along
with astonishment, curiosity and something else he couldn't
name, all in the space of the few seconds they'd taken to shake
hands. It didn't make sense.

The desire, sure. She was a very attractive woman. But
the rest of it he didn't remotely understand. He let go of her
hand with a tug of reluctance and repeated clumsily, "Yeah,
Nate."

"In that case, I'm Lannie..."

"Lannie," he echoed, still struggling with...something.

"...if you want."

Oh, I want!

In thirty seconds of acquaintance, she'd thrown him totally off course, unsettled him down to his bones, kicked a whole raft of assumptions out from under him.

Changed his life.

Except that was insane, because his life didn't work that way.

Across her cheeks, below her stunning sapphire eyes and beneath a translucent sheen of make-up, he could see the scouring remnants of wind burn and what looked like a mosquito bite. She didn't have an ounce of excess weight on her—in fact, as she'd approached across the tarmac he'd thought she was too thin for his taste—yet there was some satisfying muscle tone in those salon-tanned arms, where he'd expected the limp, boneless quality that he'd seen in models and actresses and pampered and indulged women in the past.

Even the tan wasn't quite what it seemed, at a second glance. Spray tan, definitely, but beneath it in several places— her neck and the backs of her hands—there was actual sun exposure and more of that scouring effect. She'd spent some serious time out of doors recently, and not simply lying on a Caribbean beach.

Nate thought again of what the manager of North Carolina's Sheridan Shores had told him just last week, at a corporate conference. "Atlanta Sheridan is not your stereotypical hotel heiress. If you ever meet her, don't dismiss her or underestimate her." Nate hadn't suspected then that he'd be meeting her so soon, and in such circumstances, but with an instinct that now seemed very much on the ball, he'd stored the Sheridan Shores manager's insight away in his mind, word for word.

Don't dismiss her or underestimate her.

His smug, rock-like confidence that she wouldn't last a month as manager of the Sheridan Lakes resort developed several hairline cracks, and the powerful sense of desire and deeper meaning was like an attack of vertigo when he'd never been scared of heights in his life.

"Do you have any checked bags?" he asked, working purely on auto-pilot now. She'd arrived on a commercial flight, but there had only been three other passengers on the small aircraft. A baggage cart that looked more like a golf buggy beetled its way toward the terminal, carrying an assortment of suitcases.

"Ohh yeah, I have bags!" She wrinkled her nose, half-grimace, half-smile, very cheeky. She drawled, with a hint of defiance, "I shopped, yesterday."

"Right." Of course she'd shopped. He was more than happy to have that particular element of the stereotype back in place. It gave him something to cling to, the way a shipwrecked man might cling to a single plank of wood.

The golf buggy arrived at the side of the building and its contents were unloaded inside. Yep, shopped alright. Following her indication, he pulled out two enormous pieces of Louis Vuitton luggage, more like steamer trunks than mere suitcases, an exotic looking overnight bag that appeared to be made of carpet, and—but this one couldn't be hers, surely?—a battered and stained hiking backpack, forty pound capacity if Nate was any judge. It had a sleeping bag roped to the bottom of it and a pair of burnt orange woollen hiking socks poking out the top.

"If I wheel, can you carry?" she said, extending the handles of the two chunks of Louis Vuitton and rolling them into position. She acted as if they were miniature poodles on gold chain leads. Then she nudged the scuffed hiking pack a few inches in his direction with the toe of her flimsy shoe.

"Uh, sure. The car's parked just outside." He glanced down at her ridiculous, impractical footwear and couldn't help adding, "So where have you come from, exactly? Your father didn't say." Hiking pack and Louis Vuitton. Wind burn and killer heels. Shopaholic with muscle tone. Something didn't gel, and the need to know more gnawed at his gut and wouldn't let him alone.

"Well, last night and the night before, at the Sheridan Central Park, but if you mean before that…" She looked at the backpack he was swinging onto his shoulders. "Eastern Turkey."

"Turkey. Right." The pack's straps were too tight for the bulk of his shoulders, but for a fifty-yard walk, it didn't seem worth adjusting them, so he shrugged them into a more comfortable position and put up with them. "Mr. Sheridan…Bill… your father…wasn't very specific. In fact, I only found out you were coming a couple of days ago."

"Yes, the trip was cut short." The Sheridan hotel heiress gave a little shiver, turned away from him and didn't give any more detail. Nate was left trying—and failing—to fill in the gaps.

He felt as if he'd narrowly escaped being side-swiped by an eighteen-wheel truck. Did she have any idea? He hoped to heck not.

This woman was most definitely not what he'd been expecting, not what he'd geared his strategy toward. For the second time this week, he'd been caught on the fly and he didn't like it one bit. He'd endured the feeling his whole life, thanks to the chaos of his family, but that didn't mean he handled it willingly. The reverse, in fact. He had a visceral dislike of having the ground pulled from under his feet.

On Monday, he'd been one hundred percent confident that he was on track to step in as manager of Sheridan Lakes by the end of this week. He'd filled the deputy manager role for almost a year, moving up to acting manager back in March while Ed was away having chemotherapy treatment, but the treatment and illness itself were taking too much of a toll,

Ed was formally stepping down—he'd been given a farewell dinner last night—and the job was supposed to be Nate's now, permanently. "I feel very confident, handing over to you, Ridgeway," Ed had said.

At least, the job *should* have been Nate's.

Two days ago, however, Bill Sheridan himself had flown into the resort by private helicopter. He did that. It wasn't unusual. He liked to keep personal tabs on the quality of his luxury resort hotels, even now that there were thirty-five of them, he seemed to get restless staying in one place for too long, and he rarely gave advance warning of his arrival.

Bill had sat Nate down at a quiet lunch table in the hotel's five-star restaurant, Lavande, and told him briskly, "The plan's changed. My daughter is coming home unexpectedly. She needs a break and a change of scene, and I'm going to put her into the management job instead. You'll get your chance, so don't think of this as a setback. You'll take over at Sheridan Turfside in six months when the top position opens up there. Meanwhile, I want you to help Atlanta…though she prefers to be called Lannie…in whatever way she needs, be her right-hand man. She has an MBA from Harvard—well, almost—and she's done several stints in our hotels across the country…"

Yeah, in between those other stints at A-list nightclubs and movie star parties in London and Hollywood, Nate had thought. He'd seen the paparazzi pictures.

"…so she has a strong head start. You're going to be impressed by my baby girl."

Yeah. Right.

"Oh, of course, Bill."

Nate had had to bite down hard on his cynicism and his disappointment. He didn't want to relocate to Sheridan Turfside in Kentucky. He liked it here, in New York's beautiful Adirondack Mountains. This hotel was bigger, more beautiful, more luxurious, more complex to run, a resort more than a hotel. And the surrounding wilderness was more to his taste than the groomed emerald green of Kentucky horse farms.

He had a love for the freedom and the space that almost amounted to a physical need. He'd built a sense of ownership here that he couldn't imagine feeling anywhere else. He'd even managed to scrape together the money for his own parcel of land, despite his mother and sister's negative effects on his bank balance.

"She's a bright, capable girl," Bill Sheridan had said, still speaking in glowing terms of his daughter. "She can handle the jump in responsibility if she has the right person easing the transition. That's you, Nathan, and I expect you to step up to the plate on this."

Maybe he hadn't bitten down on that cynicism hard enough. There'd been a note of warning in that last statement, as if he'd let some of it slip out.

"Yes, sir, of course," he'd said, infusing as much warmth and enthusiasm as he could into his voice, this time.

Then Bill's cell phone had begun to vibrate on the table top and he'd spent the rest of their lunch either taking calls, making them or apologizing for them, while Nate had been left to his own thoughts, which had reassured him in the end.

He'd seen the pictures of the Sheridan hotel heiress in the tabloids and magazines. Slipping into the first-class lounge at London Heathrow airport. Hanging on the arm of an Oscar-winning actor. Sunbathing topless on a Mediterranean yacht, the picture quality so poor that no one would have recognized her if not for the other photos taken earlier of her boarding the same vessel in Saint-Tropez.

Reading Bill Sheridan's subtext, Nate concluded that Ms. Sheridan wanted this job as therapy or, no, an *escape*. Failed love affair, maybe? Failed business venture? There'd been a rumor that she wanted to launch her own line of women's fashion. Maybe it hadn't ever gotten off the ground. Maybe her father was pushing her to settle down. Or possibly she was just bored. Whatever the truth, it seemed highly unlikely that she would last here.

Had seemed highly unlikely, until he'd seen the warmth and depth and intelligence in Lannie's blue eyes, felt the energy—and the chemistry—in her handshake, seen the battered hiking pack and identified those patches of sun and wind damage on what should have been thoroughly pampered skin.

Now, beyond the mystifying power of his desire, he felt an inkling of doubt. Maybe there was more to Lannie Sheridan's sudden appearance here than the whim of a spoiled heiress, or the expectations of a doting dad.

Nate hadn't considered that he might actively have to make the job difficult for her, force her out of it in order to secure his own position. Was he prepared to do that? Throw her in at the deep end? Fail to give her the right information? Allocate the least experienced staff for major events where she would require the most help?

His gut rebelled. He'd never operated that way, and he wasn't about to start now, even if such a strategy might offer him a degree of protection against this sudden feeling of vulnerability where Atlanta Sheridan was concerned.

No, there was only one choice. He would have to do exactly as Bill Sheridan wanted, grit his teeth, put on a smile and help this astonishing woman in every way he could.

Nathan Ridgeway didn't say much as he drove, Lannie noticed.

"Nate," he'd said.

Nate. Nathan. His name repeated over and over in her head like a phrase in a foreign language that she needed to learn by heart. A combination of sounds that had meant nothing a few minutes ago, but now held a world of significance.

Nathan.

Nate Ridgeway.

At the airport, she'd seen him as she opened the terminal door and had guessed he was her father's man, the one Dad had blithely promised would mentor her in whatever way she needed. There was nobody else waiting, so it had to be him. He was dressed about right, and he was looking at her. At this first glimpse, he'd represented her safe arrival and the ease of her transition, nothing more.

My ride to the hotel. Good. He's here.

But something had changed the moment they shook hands. She'd suddenly regretted yesterday's wild spree of shopping and salon pampering, despite how necessary and emotionally nourishing those things had felt at the time. She'd regretted choosing this outfit and these shoes, although in her Sheridan Central Park hotel room this morning, they'd seemed summery and celebratory and fun.

They said *bimbo,* though, and she wasn't, and normally she didn't mind if strangers got it wrong. It offered a kind of protection. The celebrity-obsessed tabloids gave the impression that she appeared this way a lot more often than she really did. Sometimes it was even a form of defiance—let people discover the truth if they took the time to actually get to know her—but today, meeting Nate...

In a rapid about-face of attitude, she'd deliberately given him what she privately called Handshake Number Two. Not the willowy, boneless drift of fingers she used when she wanted to match the hotel heiress stereotype, but the don't-underestimate-me clinch. Strong, brief, efficient.

He'd noticed it, too. He'd adjusted something in his thinking, she could see, and that had pleased her, but he'd set his jaw a little more squarely and he hadn't given very much away. There had been none of the fawning, eager-to-please behavior she'd experienced in some of her father's employees.

Which meant Mr. Ridgeway wasn't a push-over.

Perfect.

Neither was she.

All good, but more had happened during that handshake than she wanted him to know. She'd felt a strange surge of energy, as if she'd opened a window to a blast of cool mountain air, or heard the sudden beat and melody of a favorite song. Her heart had given a startled thump. The blood had rushed in her veins. This man was *different.* She felt it instinctively without knowing why.

In the darkened corner of a high-end nightclub at one in the morning, it would have been a very naked, sophisticated moment. They would have smiled at each other, acknowledged the attraction, maybe done something about it, enjoyed the illicit secret of it, at the very least.

In this context, however, they'd both put immediate shields in place. His were stronger and more determined than hers, she guessed. If he was attracted to her, it was the last thing he wanted, she could tell, and he'd make damned sure it didn't get in the way.

He looked more than capable of carrying her heavy hiking pack without raising a sweat or a complaint. She'd seen how easily he swung it onto his broad shoulders. And the smile he'd given her as they shook hands had been confident and… *clean,* somehow. She'd already sensed that he had his own rules, and that he played by them without deviation.

Now, she began to wonder a little more about the depths to him, and the layers. He looked a few years older than she was, she thought. She'd put him at thirty-three or thirty-four to her twenty-nine. He looked like a member of a Presidential security detail. Close-cropped dark hair, dark-lensed sunglasses, neat business shirt and tie and pants, the kind of watch on his left wrist that could probably tell him his blood pressure and heart rate along with the temperature, the altitude and the time in thousandths of a second. He had a secret service poker face much of the time, too.

On the phone last night, Dad had told her, "He'll be on call whenever you need him. He'll meet you at the airport, tell you everything you need to know. He'll mentor you. He's a smart man, an unusual man, and he'll know that his job is on the line if he doesn't make this run smoothly for you, Lannie."

"Dad!" She didn't like the red carpet treatment!

No, okay, sometimes she liked it a lot, but only on her own terms, only when she chose.

Relishing the red carpet treatment had been a part of her long quest to work out who she really was. Did she want to choose between the limited options her parents' moneyed lifestyle and expectations had offered her—corporate executive, society wife? A-list celebrity? Or was there something else? Tireless charity worker? Tree-hugging greenie? She'd tried on so many hats, and still hadn't found the one that really fit.

She'd spent half her adult life in places where Dad's money and influence had no reach, where no one even knew that she was *that* Atlanta Sheridan, the one who sometimes made the gossip pages and photo spreads, the one who three years ago had reached Number Seven on a major magazine's World's Best Dressed list, pictured in a stunning Hugo Boss gown.

In the Peace Corps, they'd just called her Lannie, as did Mom and Dad. Same at the Thai orphanage, and on the wilderness treks, and in the bar in New Zealand where she'd spent a fun six months pouring beers, hiking rugged trails and attempting to understand the local accent.

In all of that, something was still missing.

The thing she needed to decide now was whether this hotel management gig was more akin to the red carpet or the wilderness trail. Was she looking for a soft option, or a life-altering challenge, or something in between?

A challenge…

Who are you, Lannie Sheridan? You could have pretty much anything, according to Dad, so what do you actually want? Who are you, and, more importantly, who do you want to be for the rest of your life? It's time to stop trying on hats, and pick the one that fits.

This wouldn't be the first time in her life that she'd been hungry for a challenge, and sometimes challenges weren't safe. Sometimes they left you with death staring you in the face.

She felt the same shudder of fear that had ambushed her several times over the past few days, and knew she was very lucky to be here. She could so easily have been imprisoned in some nameless village on the slopes of Mount Ararat right at this moment, held hostage for reasons she hadn't understood at the time and didn't understand now. Political? Religious? Financial?

It did happen.

In this instance, the scary signals had been impossible to decode. Languages she didn't speak. Ethnic alliances and tensions too complex to learn from a guidebook. The escape had seemed miraculous, and she'd had the impression that if she or the others had put one foot wrong, their tour guide on the trek could have switched from their ally to their enemy without a moment's warning.

On the phone, she'd told her father that she didn't want special treatment, she wanted to earn the respect of the hotel staff on her own merits and she wanted to work hard, but right now she doubted her own sincerity on that. She was just so tired and wrung out.

She'd taken a lavish break after the hard-working year in Thailand. She'd flown to London to catch up with her best friend, where she'd spent two weeks gossiping, pampering and partying, before meeting the wilderness trekking tour in Istanbul. But Thailand had been tough, and two weeks of city pampering hadn't been enough, with the daily miles of mountain hiking that had immediately followed.

Maybe what she really needed, at least for a while, was simply to feel safe and cocooned in the familiar luxury of her favorite of her father's fabulous hotels. She'd love to visit the spa. Sunbathe by the pool. Read novels with splashy covers and hooky titles. Give herself time to think.

Relax, she thought. You *are* safe.

She leaned the seat back and eased her body into the soft leather of a Sheridan corporate car.

You're safe. You're safe.

The air-conditioning played a cool breeze onto her bare lower legs and the sun shone dappled onto her face as they drove past a line of leafy summer-green trees. Nate Ridgeway was taking the back roads from the airport, but she knew them all. Sheridan Lakes was one of the first hotels in the Sheridan hotels chain, and she'd spent half her childhood summers up here, hiking the mountain trails, swimming in the lakes and streams. Soon they would come to the road that skirted the biggest of the lakes, past the motels and cottages and luxury waterfront lodges with their wooden docks and moored boats. Then, on a stretch of forested land jutting out so that the lake surrounded it on three sides, would be the hotel.

You're safe here.

With her eyes closed, she said lazily to the man beside her, "So do I get a week or two off before I start?"

She still had calluses on her heels and the sides of her feet from the hiking boots. Pretty, celebratory designer shoes did not normally make allowances for such things, and her feet were killing her. She'd lost weight in the humid heat of Thailand, and several more pounds had dropped off during that endless-seeming trek through the darkness on Mount Ararat, with only a couple of protein bars and a water bottle to keep her going for more than thirty-six hours.

There was a moment's silence, then, "Sure you do."

"You're *not* sure."

"I'm here to make this whole experience whatever you want it to be."

Very diplomatic of him. Very smooth, in that deep, rough-edged voice. But the words were wrong, and she knew she was partly to blame. She opened her eyes, sat the seat back up to near vertical again, tried a light approach, with a smile in her voice. "You make it sound as if the whole job, the whole management position, is nothing more than a vacation, or a whim."

"Well…" He paused, as if trying to decide how much to say, how honest to be. "Isn't it true? Isn't that what you want?"

She took a sideways glance in his direction, and once again that complex blast of feeling slammed into her. He might be attracted to her, but he didn't fully approve of her—okay, she couldn't totally blame him, there—and he wasn't afraid to let it show.

It suddenly occurred to her that Dad had probably dumped him in the dirt with this whole idea of her managing the hotel, since Nate Ridgeway himself had been acting manager for the past three months.

Shoot, why hadn't she thought about this possibility before? Of course Dad had dumped him in the dirt. She loved her parents, but recognized their powerful combination of ruthlessness and entitlement when it came to their baby girl. Dad wouldn't have thought twice about kicking a top-flight manager out of his position at a moment's notice in order to make space for her.

No wonder there was a degree of steely reserve in this guy.

She shouldn't have let Dad do it, but she'd been so homesick and wrung out, she hadn't had the power to think, hadn't had the space. Everything had happened so fast. She'd first called home from the scruffy *pansiyon* in Dogubayazit where they'd fetched up just a few nights ago.

She'd burst into tears of exhaustion and spent adrenaline, and when Dad had asked, "Are you coming home?" she'd said, in the emotional heat of the moment, yes, *yes,* she was coming home, and she never wanted to leave again, she wanted to settle to something, it was time, it had been so great, all the things she'd done, the travel and work in out of the way places, even the silly stuff, the nightclubs and parties, but she was done, she wanted a real career now, a settled life in a place she loved, something to justify the Harvard business degree Dad had funded for her, and which she might go on to actually finish now.

"Really?"

"I'm only three credits short. I know you were disappointed when I dropped out..."

And hey presto, Dad had fixed it on her behalf, at her favorite Sheridan hotel.

Now, she felt ashamed, angry with herself and her father. She should have given herself more time, should have recognized that it was her fear and homesickness talking, and so should he. He shouldn't try to fix things for her so automatically, and with such a limited repertoire of solutions. And why, oh, why, had she mentioned that damned degree?

Nate drove with smooth attention to detail as glinting stretches of lake flashed past, looking as if he'd never had anything fixed for him by anyone else in his life. He was totally self-made. She wasn't sure how she knew this with such certainty. Just a hardness to him, perhaps, and a kind of stoic reserve, through which had slipped those occasional traces of disapproval that he couldn't fully conceal.

It was a little scary to think that he was going to be her mentor.

Scary for reasons she didn't want to explore too much.

"Can we talk about this straight up?" she asked. "Full honesty, no corporate line?"

He didn't look at her, had his eyes fixed on the road. "Sure." His stock answer, outwardly accommodating, but with a sub-text. She needed to get past that.

"Can you stop the car?"

"Right now?"

"Yes. Pull over right here."

Silently, he slowed and curved out to the narrow verge of the road, stopped the vehicle and opened the windows. The lake twinkled between a stand of pine trees, and across a stretch of water you could see the hotel. It was a classic Victorian-era construction restored to pristine luxury, with its terraces and function rooms, its separate lodges dotted amongst the pines, and its lush gardens sloping down to the boat docks at the water's edge.

The sight of it was so familiar and well-loved, Lannie could have cried.

So peaceful.

So beautiful.

This was the one thing she was certain that she'd gotten right—coming here, where she'd always felt grounded. The woodsy scent of pine and moss came richly through the car windows and she just wanted to breathe it in. Just that. Breathe in this familiar, beloved air for about two weeks before she even thought of anything else.

But she knew if she did that, she would lose Nathan Ridgeway's respect and once lost—maybe she'd even lost it already—it was something she might never get back, and for some reason the idea of losing it made her feel bereft in spirit, down to her bones.

"Look at me, Nate."

"I am."

"Yeah, well, the sunglasses don't give much away." He was

half looking at her. The rest of his attention lay on the narrow, bendy road which cars regularly took too fast. She guessed he wasn't too happy about parking a near-new Sheridan corporate vehicle on such a narrow stretch of verge. Not too happy, either, about the fact that they were seated so close without the safety of movement or crowds.

Fine. She didn't plan on making this a lengthy interview.

"No, I don't want a vacation," she said. "I may take things a little easier for the first couple of days. I'm pretty tired, for reasons I won't go into right now. But after that, you can throw me in at the deep end and I promise you I'll swim."

"The pool is very nice," he drawled. "I'll show you where it is when we arrive."

"That's not what I meant, and you know it. And I've been swimming in that pool since I was five."

"Sorry."

"Hmm, really? Are you?"

He sighed between his teeth, lifted his sunglasses so she could see his eyes. They were dark, speculative and as cynical as she'd expected. "I was attempting some humor. It didn't work, and I probably shouldn't have tried. The bottom line is, since you apparently want some honesty, you're Atlanta Sheridan. You can do anything you want and you know that. You're not exactly going to get fired for not meeting performance objectives."

"I'm not looking for special treatment, if that's what you're suggesting. Or asking. Can we get that clear right now? This job is real for me. My performance objectives—my own personal performance objectives, even if they're not Dad's or yours—are real."

"But you want to start with days off." One arm rested on the steering wheel, the way it might rest around a woman's shoulders. His hands were large but lean. Hardworking hands. Dad had mentioned in passing that Nate had worked his way up in the Sheridan Empire from the very bottom rung. No Cornell degree in hotel admin for him, just a long ladder and a determined push.

"I've just flown halfway round the world," she heard herself say. "I'm tired."

"Cattle-class, right?"

Okay, it had sounded whiney and spoiled, and indeed she'd flown first-class.

It wasn't the flying that had exhausted her, it was the dislocation of transitting from an isolated Turkish village to a five-star Manhattan hotel in a day and a half. It was the three weeks of trekking in the Kars and Toros Mountains before that, on top of the year of volunteer work in Thailand. Most of all, however, it was the thirty-six hours of sheer, naked fear on the slopes of Mount Ararat, but she didn't want to tell him about this, because she knew that putting the whole experience into words would bring it back too vividly.

"Take me seriously," she said, with something of the grit she'd so recently needed coloring her voice.

"Then take yourself seriously." His gaze raked over her and she felt the heat of his challenge and disapproval. Something else, too. Couldn't possibly be curiosity or respect. "We have our biggest wedding of the year the day after tomorrow, first weekend in June, with the rehearsal dinner tomorrow night. Four hundred guests. Celebrities, politicians, people in single digits on the Forbes rich list. Personal friends of yours, some of them, I've been told. Virtually the whole hotel is booked out for it. If you do want to actually *work* in this job—"

"Haven't I convinced you yet that I want to work?"

He ignored her interruption. "You'll be there, dressed to the nines, smiling, schmoozing and helping me make sure there's not a detail out of place."

"Right."

"Are you in?"

"I'm in."

"So can I get out of this death-trap parking place you insisted on, and back onto the road?"

"Sure," she answered with heavy emphasis, mocking his own use of the word earlier.

Five minutes later, he pulled up outside her new home, one of the luxury two-bedroom, two-level lodges that formed part of the hotel's extensive resort development. "Final word on the subject, before I bring your bags in?"

"Final? Really?"

"For now."

"Go ahead."

"If you want to work on this wedding, report for duty in the terrace bar at five-thirty this afternoon and I'll talk you through it."

"I'll be there."

"And, uh…" The gravel was back in his voice. "Thanks for being up-front, just now. Good that we both know where we stand."

"That's what I thought, yes."

But did they know where they stood? Really?

There was that something in the air again, even more expectant than before and even more dangerous. It made Lannie's breath catch in her chest, suddenly, as Nate climbed out of the car and went around to the trunk. She didn't know if she wanted to work with a man like this—a man who affected her like this—or if she'd rather run a mile before he got to her too badly. There was a fine line between his respect and his condemnation, and again she was torn.

Did she care what he thought of her? Did it matter if they were colleagues, lovers or friends? Or could he go jump in the lake, because, after all, she was Daddy's girl and there were countless options for an easy way out?

Chapter Three

"Dad?"

"Lannie! You're calling from the Lakes?"

"Yes, I'm here, everything's fine. I've unpacked, and I'm about to hit the pool."

"Nathan Ridgeway was waiting for you at the airport?"

"On the dot."

"Yes, he's a good man."

"But listen…" She walked over to the window of her upstairs lodge bedroom. Two pine trees stood sentinel just outside, a breeze sighing through their thick green needles. Between them she could see the rose garden in full summer bloom and beyond it the circular driveway and front entrance of the hotel. Nate himself stood there greeting some guests. Important ones, from the look of them, an older couple and another man, possibly members of the bridal party at the upcoming wedding. "You shouldn't have done it, Dad."

"Done what?"

"Bumped Nathan from his position so that I could fill it instead."

"Is that what he told you?"

"He didn't have to, not in so many words." She could see Nate laughing at something one of the male guests had said. He looked at his watch, cheerfully answered a question he'd probably been asked a thousand times. "I know you, Father dear, and I could read between the lines. I wasn't looking for special—" She broke off and amended more honestly, "I guess I was perfectly happy to have the special treatment, but not at someone else's expense."

Not at Nathan Ridgeway's expense.

Now he was gesturing toward the grounds, talking about the extensive facilities, Lannie guessed. One of the men clapped him on the shoulder, then the guests disappeared inside. An Italian sports car circled into the entrance and once again Nate was on alert, smiling and stepping forward. Lannie was quite certain he must have far more important things to do than this, but his body language gave no sign of it as he helped a gorgeous young woman—the bride-to-be?—out of the front passenger seat.

"If he makes things difficult for you in any way, honey—"

"Dad... That's not the point. You didn't have to put me directly into the top job here. You could have slotted me into something less demanding, where I could have handled it out of my own experience and not needed a baby-sitter."

"You won't need him for long."

"And where I wasn't bumping someone else from a position he quite rightly considered his."

The parking attendant took the keys of the Italian sports car and drove off. When the new arrivals weren't looking, Nate flicked another glance at his watch. He definitely had more important things to do. Then his cell phone rang. He looked at the number on the screen, obviously made an apology to the arriving couple, said something to the bellboy and stepped away from the front entrance to take the call with a degree of privacy. His shoulders looked tighter, suddenly, and he hunched his back and put a hand over one ear as if to shield both himself and the caller at the other end of the line from the outside world.

"Your last name is Sheridan, honey," Dad said in her ear. "I'm not going to put you on the night shift at the front desk. How is that going to be good for staff relations?"

He didn't get it. He never would. She loved him and she wanted to make him happy. She didn't want to turn her back completely on the Sheridan heritage he'd built for her, but why was his vision for her future so limited? How could she find her own way without busting out of the family mold with a violence she didn't want?

She would put herself on the night shift at the front desk if she had to, she decided, in order to prove herself to Nate. She wanted to carve her own way in life, make her own mistakes, her own decisions, her own bounce-backs if she got it wrong, and surely it shouldn't all have to be such a big deal. There had to be another option, a middle ground.

With a sigh, she asked after Mom, told Dad that the new decor in the lodge was gorgeous, ended their conversation and flipped her phone onto the bedside table. In making things work with Nathan Ridgeway at Sheridan Lakes, it seemed as if she was on her own, and that was good.

And if she couldn't make it work, then she could do what she and the trek group had done—no other choice—on the slopes of Mount Ararat.

Bail.

Fast.

Without a backward glance.

* * *

In his ear, Nate heard the breathy imitation of Marilyn Monroe singing him happy birthday. It was his mother, remembering his birthday two days late.

"Hi, Mom," he said, steeling himself as usual.

"Hi, sweetheart, did you like the impression?"

"It was very good. I mean, I knew who it was."

"Is that all you can say? That you knew who it was?" She sounded upbeat, impatient and expectant, which meant she had some news. This was never good. "Cole thinks it's pitch-perfect, and that I have the mannerisms and her whole personality down perfect, too. And I've been working on Diana Ross and Dolly Parton and a few others."

"Who is Cole?"

"My agent."

"When did you get an agent?"

"You're saying that as if I haven't been a professional singer your whole life. I've had a ton of agents."

He managed not to suggest that this was part of the problem—a ton of agents, all of them bad—and avoided pointing out that the word *professional* traditionally indicated some actual earning power. He'd earned more from his morning paper route at the age of ten than Mom had ever earned from her singing, yet she put "Singer" under the "Occupation" heading on every tax and census and banking form she ever filled out, the way his sister Krystal put "Actress and model" with similar dodgy justification.

He tried to form the words to congratulate his mother on having a new agent, as if this wasn't step one on a familiar path to disaster, but he just couldn't do it.

"We're going to open a bar," she said. "As a stepping stone."

"A bar?"

"With live music. Me, doing my impressions. And guest artists twice a week."

"Where?" His best hope was that the plan would never get off the ground. It was the plans that did get off the ground but then crashed back down before they reached the end of the runway that created the real problems. And since when did running your own bar count as a stepping stone? It was a major commitment, all on its own.

"Oh, we'll construct a stage area," Mom was saying, her voice alight with the brightness of the dream. "There's plenty of space for it. We'll only have to lose a few of the tables."

"I mean what part of the country?"

"San Diego."

"San Diego. Is that where Cole is from?"

"No, he's from Tulsa, but he's been working out of L.A. for the past five years and the city is just impossible now. He wants to think strategically on this, and go for a less crowded market. We've found the perfect place and signed a five-year lease. We're moving down there this weekend, to get started on the refit."

"Wait a minute, already signed? Five years? You haven't—"

"See? This is why I haven't said anything to you before this. I knew you'd try to talk me out of it if I told you any of the details before it was locked in. That's why I'm late with your birthday call. We finalized the paperwork today."

"Look, I would only try to talk you out of it if the figures didn't stack up." He would *want* to talk her out of it, no matter what, but he'd only *try* if he had some solid data to back up his case. Even then, he knew she wouldn't listen. "Do they stack up?"

"Of course they do!"

"Have you done a feasibility study? Looked at your nearest competitors? Run your figures past an accountant?"

"We've taken out a loan," she answered, as if this covered his questions.

"A business loan? From a bank?" He felt a cautious degree of relief. If a bank, with its tightened restrictions on lending, had examined their plans and been prepared to support them, then maybe the figures did stack up.

"Well, yes, from a bank. A personal loan. Half in Cole's name and half in mine. Two loans, I guess. They should cover the whole cost of the remodel and we'll go from there."

"Personal loans." The relief evaporated.

Personal loans didn't attract the kind of scrutiny given to commercial loans and mortgages, and they had higher interest rates. Personal loans were for buying a Jacuzzi or a flat-screen TV, not for sinking into a demanding business venture with major ongoing overheads and no guarantee of a profit. He thought about giving her a lecture on the subject.

Any business venture should start out with enough capital to cover a full year of operating costs. There should be a full budget prepared, an analysis of the market, contingency plans for unexpected setbacks. Did she have any idea of the working hours that went into running a bar? Two modest-size personal loans wouldn't be anywhere near enough to cover the ongoing risk. The only upside was that at least the numbers weren't crippling in scale.

"The lease—" he began.

"See, again you're going to rain on my parade—oh, I'm doing Barbra Streisand, too, of course, I forgot to say. But you know I'd never leave out Barbra."

"I'm not raining on your parade, I'm just making sure you've asked the right questions. You couldn't have gotten a shorter lease?"

"Yes, but there's a discount on the longer one. In the long run, it'll save us money. See? Cole is on top of this, Nate. I can't wait for you to meet him."

Which meant he wasn't just her agent, he was her boyfriend, too.

Again, it was a familiar story. Nate felt his temples tighten and his jaw wire itself shut. Attempting to wind up this call without any more reproaches from his mother, he wondered how long until the next one—the one where she wanted him to wire her money, just to tide things over. Or would it be the one where she was in tears because she and Cole had broken up but not before he'd swindled her?

As he shoved his phone into a pocket he closed the door in his mind marked *Family* the way he might have closed the door on a closet crammed with junk. Just ignore it, put it off, get it out of sight.

He couldn't afford to deal with the contents of the closet, right now. It was one o'clock on a Thursday. He had a big society wedding for four hundred guests to navigate over the next three days, and technically he wasn't even in charge anymore. Would Atlanta Sheridan insist on making last-minute changes purely to show everyone who was in the top job here? Would that unwanted slam of attraction and bone-deep interest that had hit him at the airport please be considerate enough to leave him the heck alone...?

Mom's problems would have to wait. He cleared the granite steps running up to the front entrance in a single loping step and plunged into four hours of nonstop work, without so much as a banana for lunch.

And would Atlanta Sheridan show for their wedding rundown?

In hindsight, Nate questioned his choice of a meeting place. Five-thirty in the terrace bar on a warm June afternoon sounded a little too much like a date. When he entered, five minutes early, the sliding French windows had been opened up, a pianist had begun to play unobtrusive jazz classics, and the place was filled with tanned men and bare-shouldered women, laughing and talking over summery cocktails and cold beer.

The Adirondacks weren't always this sunny and warm at this time of the year, by any means, but it seemed that even the weather smiled upon Atlanta Sheridan's changes of plan.

In the event, too, he'd had to snatch this window in his schedule, which had been complicated by the fact that the strawberries supplied for tomorrow's rehearsal dinner dessert were of such poor quality that they couldn't be used, and Head Chef Michel Saint-Gilles was rightly insisting that fresh ones be brought in. They'd been having problems with two of their produce suppliers since April.

If the Sheridan heiress kept him waiting…

She didn't.

Here she was, on the dot of five-thirty, and he wondered if the scrupulous punctuality was a statement of some kind. If so, he appreciated it, especially after the phone conversation with his mother, who had never been on time for anything in her life.

He hadn't yet made up his mind if he was going to be mentoring a down-to-earth, hard-working team player this summer or a spoiled, high-maintenance brat. It could go either way, at this stage, and he knew that he'd be the one accommodating whatever image Lannie Sheridan chose to present.

She looked stunning, he couldn't help noticing, in a soft, figure-hugging dress splashed with summer color. He wished he could manage not to notice. And she smelled even better, a fresh powdery smell without the cloying sweetness of vanilla and fruit which he detested on a woman's skin.

"What are you drinking?" he asked her, after they'd exchanged a brief greeting.

"Mineral water, with a twist." She'd wasted no time on the choice, and had opened a small spiral-bound notebook.

Shouldn't it be a BlackBerry? "I'm sure you want to get started. You must have a million things to do. I'll work by hand and input the important stuff later." She flashed him a crooked smile that said she knew he was questioning the notebook. "I can't think on a screen. It gives me motion sickness."

Motion sickness on electronic screens, but she regularly flew long-haul flights across major oceans. Another contradiction that a part of him clamored to explore.

Suppressing the inconvenient feeling, he handed her a binder filled with printed sheets in plastic sleeves. "Look through this, first. Schedule, menu, seating plan, cell numbers for the important staff. Plus a couple of very confidential pages about specialized guest requirements. A few other things. You'll see."

"What exactly do I need to do tomorrow?" She didn't look up at him as she spoke. Her head was bent over the binder, balanced on her knees, her blond hair fell in a soft curve against her cheek, and she studied each page with total focus.

"Check the guest list in advance for people you know personally. Make sure you give them the right touch."

"Glorified party hostess?" She gave him a wry look, but he managed to stay unmoved.

"You want to polish wineglasses, your rate of pay will drop quite a lot. You want backroom executive management, I'll need to look over your accounting qualifications. Let's go with your natural strengths to start with, okay?"

"Fair enough." She began to look through the guest list, eyebrows rising at several of the names. She murmured, "Mmm, so he's not married to Carla anymore, I didn't know that…" and, "I don't think these two are speaking to each other. Did the bride tell you? It's recent. Hope they're not seated too close."

"Let me see."

"These two." She pointed.

He checked the seating plan. Adjacent tables. Damn. It wasn't the first time tomorrow's bride had neglected to give an important update on some rather complex family politics. "I'll have to call their wedding planner and work out how we can tweak the table positions. Clearly she hasn't been told, either. Thanks for that."

"Just going with my natural strength." It could easily have been a cutting line, but she softened it with another unexpected grin and he found himself grinning back, hypnotized by the life in her eyes, the grace in her body. If nothing else, she was...refreshing.

Yes, that was the right word. She was like mint toothpaste or mountain air or a smooth dive into a cool but sunny pool.

Two things happened. First, his body told him yet again in simple, male and very certain terms that he was attracted to her—to the honed yet pampered blond-and-tan body, to the mix of mischief and entitlement, to the quick, energetic mind. Second, his head told him that messing with the big boss's daughter was the last thing in the world he should consider doing when he was supposed to be her mentor in the management role and nothing more.

If there was anything more to his feelings, it was only his very private hope that she wouldn't last in the job.

Make that three things.

Third thing, she read what was happening to him. Saw it somehow in the way he shifted in the low-slung lounge seating, or in how he had to clear his throat and look away. He waited, on edge.

So she'd read it. Now, how would she react? Lord, he hadn't been sure before. That first time at the airport. Closeted with her in the car at the side of the road. This time he knew he'd given himself away. Hell, he didn't want her to freeze up and go running to Daddy with the news that he was coming on to her. He wanted her to start flirting with him even less. There had to be a middle ground, another choice.

Was there a middle ground?

He looked down at the binder and flicked a couple of pages, not sure what he was even pretending to look for. In his peripheral vision, he was able to see her face and was astonished to discover a blush on her cheeks. Turkish mountain windburn? He didn't think so. And she was smiling. Just a small smile, soft and secret and almost innocent, kind of dizzy, as if she liked what was happening to both of them, liked the idea that he found her attractive but she didn't plan on doing anything about it—wouldn't be using it to her advantage.

Or not yet, anyhow…

He felt a light-headed rush of relief. Sheesh, she had the power to make him the most miserable man in the world, in this job of taking care of her. If she didn't intend to do that, then he was very thankful indeed.

"You probably have more you need to do," she said, and for both of them it was a safe line, an easy out.

"Yes, I have six more meetings tonight with various staff."

"Do you want me to sit in?"

"Save your energy for tomorrow and Saturday."

She gave a little nod and he realized that what she'd said this morning about being tired was the pure truth. Beyond the immaculate packaging, she looked as if she was only just holding it together, and his respect for her rose another notch. He'd challenged her commitment to the new role and she hadn't punished him for it. It seemed instead as if she was punishing herself.

"You look hungry, too," he added. "Can I send some room service over to your lodge? Or there should be a room-service menu in the binder by the lodge phone, if you want to order for yourself."

"Would you send something?" She tipped her head to the side like a little girl. "I couldn't even make a decision, right now. Soup and salad. Something I don't need to chew."

"You're really wiped. What happened on your trip?"

His jaw almost dropped to his chest when she told him— that her trekking group had narrowly escaped being taken hostage by an unidentified clutch of armed mountain bandits on the slopes of Mount Ararat, that they'd been on the move, on foot, for thirty-six hours straight, in order to reach the safety of a friendly village, that she'd never been sure whether their guide was really on their side, and had only begun to breathe easily when her flight to the U.S. took off from the airport in Istanbul.

Hell, and he'd openly questioned her commitment when she'd suggested some time off before she started!

"I'm so sorry," he told her, the words completely inadequate. "You should have said. Given me the details right away."

"I couldn't. It's not fun to talk about. It takes me back into it. I thought you might not want me screaming and shaking and crying all over you, in the car at the side of the road. And I didn't especially want to generate more nightmares for myself, either. The shopping spree in New York helped a little. I'm thinking if I go on wearing really impractical shoes for the next week, I'll start to forget." She was mocking herself, making him smile, when really he felt aghast.

"I'm really sorry."

"It's okay." She gave a pretty shrug. "I've told you now."

"Take the time off."

"I don't want to. You're right. I need to jump in at the deep end. I'm pretty hopeless at lazing around."

"I'm really—"

"It's done. It's finished. It's fine. I'll open my windows tonight, and get a really good sleep. It's a gorgeous bedroom, right up amongst the scent of pine needles, and it's cosy. Was it you who assigned me that lodge?"

"Your dad said you should have one of the lodges." He still felt as if she'd given him a blow to the head. How did she keep doing this? How was he going to protect himself against more of the same? "Uh, I thought it made sense for it to be as close as possible to the hotel, rather than right on the lakefront, farther away, even though those lodges are larger."

"Well, thank you. It was a great choice. There's enough space here with the grounds and the lake and the mountains, I don't need it indoors. And, as I said, the air will help me sleep. When do you need me in the morning?"

"Whenever you're ready. Take tomorrow—"

"No. It's fine. I'll find you?"

"Around. Ask at the front desk. Someone will know."

They smiled at each other once more, their new partnership deepening a little, while in Nate the knocked-off-balance feeling began to subside. He still didn't know what to think about her, from a professional point of view, how much to trust the quite stunning positive signs he'd seen so far.

That first glimpse of her walking across the tarmac this morning already seemed like weeks ago, and his smug confidence that she'd be easy to handle a piece of massive naivety on his part. When was the last time he'd felt this vulnerable, this out of his depth? Even with the worst of his family's crises, he had a greater sense of control.

And together he and the Sheridan heiress had to manage the biggest wedding of the Sheridan Lakes year.

Chapter Four

Pieces of mashed and crumbled wedding cake lay on white and gold plates waiting to be cleared away. The bride and groom had just departed in a chaotic blend of rattling tin cans, sprayed shaving cream and whooping cheers. The open bar was still doing a brisk business—a little too brisk in the case of some patrons. Lannie kept a discreet but watchful eye on the bride's new uncle-in-law, Barry Morgan. She knew he had bought his way out of a serious sexual harassment lawsuit a few years ago after a drunken "error of judgment" with a member of the catering staff at another equally lavish family wedding.

It was almost midnight, and the only thing keeping her on her feet was the knowledge that she'd done a good job, and that the shoes would have to come off eventually if she put enough muscle into the problem. She'd worked a total of thirty-two hours since yesterday morning, fully dressed for the role. From the perspective of the sixteen-member bridal party and the four hundred guests, the wedding had gone without a hitch, but in the restaurant kitchens, back offices, delivery docks and staff-only corridors of the hotel there had been some near-disasters.

Lannie wasn't convinced that either Nate or the Head Chef had slept at all.

"Still here?" asked a voice close to her. Nate himself. "I told you to leave an hour ago."

"See that bald man with the paunch?"

"I see about six of them."

"The one propping up the bar."

"Okay, now we're down to two."

"The one on the left."

"Gotcha. Mr. Morgan. Barry."

"That's him. And see the girl picking up the empties?"

"Mmm, and now I see the man with the paunch leering at the girl picking up the empties. Is that really why you haven't left? Is it that serious? Morgan's a sleaze, I can see that, but he's just looking."

"I have inside information." She told him about the lawsuit, the damning evidence and the payoff on the quiet.

"I'd have handled it myself if you'd told me."

"You had other priorities." There had been a problem with the rock-hard frosting on the cake, and a fistfight between two of the cooks in the kitchen. "And maybe if he'd left the bar four drinks ago..."

"But he didn't."

And now he was making his move, his bleary eyes fixed hungrily on the waitress's black-trousered derriere, his hand already stretched out in a curve, and his exit route clear, through an unobtrusive nearby door and down a flight of stairs. Lannie had found him earlier in the day inspecting the staff-only section of the hotel at the bottom of those stairs, a windowless corridor running at basement level between the delivery dock and the least formal of the hotel's three eating establishments. He wasn't just a drunken oaf, he planned his "lapses" in advance.

Lannie watched Nate fire himself across the ballroom like a bullet from a silenced gun, smooth, fast and deadly. He intercepted the girl and her tray first, gesturing toward a distant table scattered with glasses. Then he mowed down the drunken man, steering him off course while he introduced himself, asked about the guest's comfort, and his needs for tomorrow. Would Mr. Morgan like to arrange a boat charter? A scenic helicopter flight?

She could only guess at the actual words. The band was still playing for the somewhat sagging cluster of dancing guests. Barry looked confused, then annoyed, then distracted and finally flattered at the attention. Nate magically removed the half-empty brandy glass from his hand without him even noticing. They reached the broad doorway that led from the ballroom to the lobby and disappeared. Nate intended to walk the man all the way to the elevator and send him up to his room, Lannie understood. She expected he'd then take a detour to the security room for a few words with the night staff.

The waitress didn't have a clue what a narrow escape she'd had, just as the guests didn't know that the police had arrested both of the brawling cooks, or that the whipped cream on the wedding cake was a last-minute switch in the kitchen once the slate-hard frosting had been chipped off. Lannie had made a mental note not to outsource the hotel's large-scale baking to Gloria Dawn's Cakes for All Occasions next time around, and wondered if it had been Nate's decision to do so for this wedding.

She eased herself into a chair and watched the remaining couples and clusters on the dance floor, her feeling of fatigue a pleasant one now that the event was winding down. She'd enjoyed the frantic activity, the lavish celebration and the interaction with the guests far more than she'd expected to.

She'd enjoyed the interaction with Nate Ridgeway, too. Beyond the endless To Do list, there'd been an instinctive teamwork between the two of them that she hadn't expected—that could have been a little scary if she stopped to think about it—and she understood why everyone on the hotel staff seemed to treat him with warmth and respect.

It had been a truly beautiful wedding, and the aura of love and romance still hung in the air, more powerful than the mingled scents of perfume and chocolate and wine. Now, an older man and woman swayed to the slow number, smiling at each other. A nerdy looking young man held an attractive redhead like fragile porcelain in his arms, as if unable to believe his luck. She seemed equally smitten. Like many of the women on the dance floor, she'd taken off her impractical heels and was dancing in bare feet. The eight-piece band, fronted by a big name Broadway singer, had been brought up from New York City on very lucrative terms, so they were happy, too.

Nate appeared again. "None of them seem to want to stop dancing, but they all look pretty harmless. Why are you still here?"

"Grabbing a moment to unwind."

"It'd be quieter in your lodge."

"I love the dancing." She loved watching it as much as taking part, especially the slow numbers like this one, late in a wedding banquet, when you could see seasoned married couples falling in love all over again, and young singles discovering for the first time how well they melded together in each other's arms.

"Weddings," Nate commented lightly. "Bring out the best and the worst, don't they?"

"Always!"

"Oh, Mr. Ridgeway!" One of the bride's aunts had come up to him, hovering at the edge of his short exchange with Lannie. "I wanted to thank you for sending out to the drugstore for replacement medication for my husband. That was so good of you. We both panicked when we discovered he'd forgotten to pack it. I was so flustered, you must have thought me very foolish."

"Not at all, Mrs. Braithwaite."

"And Atlanta, my dear, it's wonderful to see you following in your father's footsteps. This has always been my favorite of the Sheridan hotels."

She smiled at the older woman. "Mine, too. How can you beat the setting?"

"And somehow your parents always manage to maintain such a wonderful personal touch."

"It's a priority for both of them, but Sheridan Lakes has been in Nathan's hands for the past three months so you must give him the credit tonight."

"Oh, I do! But I haven't seen you dancing this evening, Atlanta."

"I'm not here as a guest, Mrs. Braithwaite."

"Oh, does that really matter this late in the evening? You just said to Mr. Ridgeway how much you love it."

"I'm not sure that my feet would love it tonight, though." She lifted her foot to show a cruelly impractical shoe. Nate drew in a sharp breath as if he, too, was feeling the bite of fatigue, if not in his feet then everywhere else.

"Honey, if my sister can take off her shoes at her own daughter's wedding, then so can you," Barbara Braithwaite said. She looked at the dance floor and then around the tables, clearly in search of a suitable dance partner. There were none. Before Lannie could distract her from the idea, she'd turned to Nate. "Mr. Ridgeway, *do* take this lovely young woman onto the dance floor. You've earned some downtime, too, as much as she has."

"If she wants me to…"

"Of course she wants you to, and look at her other choices for a partner!"

Indeed, the pickings were thin. There was a fifteen-year-old boy whose attention was fixed on the electronic gamer in his hands, a cluster of guys talking loudly about money and stocks in a way that suggested they'd had too much to drink, and several elderly men parked very firmly in their seats.

"Kick your shoes off, Lannie," Mrs. Braithwaite ordered.

"I may need a tire iron to pry them loose."

But in fact she slipped them off easily, while Nate stood watching her with a wry expression on his face. In the line of duty he'd already managed about a hundred different tasks today, and a thousand and one details. Dancing with the Sheridan heiress at the biggest wedding of the year was apparently just one more.

On the dance floor, the couples shifted position and tempo as "Close To You" gave way to "The Way We Were." Barbara Braithwaite practically arranged Nate's arms around Lannie's waist and shoulder and pushed them toward an unoccupied stretch of the dance floor. She then hauled Mr. Braithwaite into place, as if Nate and Lannie needed to follow a good example.

"I'm not sure about this song," Lannie said, because conversation was a little easier than silence, standing so close to him, moving with his rhythm. She would have preferred something with a faster tempo, with Nate Ridgeway as a partner.

"Easy to dance to," he pointed out. "Too slow to get wrong."

He shifted his hand to a slightly different angle against her waist. If the song was easy to dance to, then he was easy to dance *with,* she decided. Part of his professional repertoire, probably. This wouldn't be the first time dancing had been required of him at a big hotel function. Maybe he'd even had lessons…

No, she decided as the song continued. No lessons. He wasn't really dancing, just swaying and stepping, going through the motions. His body had a natural rhythm and strength. She didn't have to fear a heavy foot on her sore toes. But his mind was elsewhere.

"What are you thinking about, Nate?"

"Just the song."

"I can't believe you like it. I would have thought it far too sentimental for a man."

His laugh acknowledged the point. "I've heard it enough, for sure." It was a cryptic line, but he didn't explain it.

She could feel a new tension in him and began to pull away. Beyond the smooth performance, he didn't really want to be here, doing this, she could tell. He let her go without a protest, stepping back and wiping his hand around his neck, above the collar of his shirt, as if trying to soften stress-tightened muscles.

"I think that's it for the dancing," she said lightly, not wanting him to think that she cared about their early finish. The band hadn't even yet hit the high point of the song. "Though Mrs. Braithwaite will be disappointed in us."

"I've just remembered a couple of things. But let me walk you to your lodge, first."

"There's no need."

"I want to talk about what's next for you." He put a hand light on her upper arm and steered her away from the dancers. Sure enough, she saw Barbara Braithwaite crane her head over her husband's shoulder and frown. Finished already? But they made such a lovely couple!

"What's next?" Lannie echoed, after shrugging an apology to Mrs. Braithwaite.

"These past two days haven't exactly been typical of your workload," Nate answered, "even if we do have weddings here every weekend until the end of September. We need to have a proper meeting in the main office, with computers and spreadsheets right in front of us, so I can talk you through the decisions that need making over the next couple of weeks, the menu Chef Saint-Gilles is suggesting for fall, the supply accounts that aren't working as well as they should. We've had problems with our fresh produce this summer, for example."

They left the ballroom. The lobby was very quiet at this hour, a cool, gracious expanse of polished wood and stone. Outside, the air had cooled to the delicious freshness Lannie loved in these mountains. They walked in silence across the curved and brick-paved driveway, through the rose gardens and the pine trees to the front of her lodge.

"First thing Monday morning, then, I guess," she suggested to Nate.

"Ten o'clock? I already have a couple of breakfast meetings scheduled before that."

"Ten o'clock is good."

"Take tomorrow for yourself, then."

"I will, thanks." She hesitated, frustrated about the way they'd begun to deal with each other, the way they'd pulled back and put layers of protection in place. He was so reserved and cool and formal. He gave so little away. The prickle of something in the air could have been the budding of distrust or dislike, but she didn't think so. On the closer acquaintance they'd developed over the past two days she didn't dislike him. Not at all.

She just wanted—

What?

To crack through the shell. To understand him a little better, maybe. To find out if she'd only imagined those first moments of curiosity about each other, and those more primal and powerful moments of desire.

She hadn't imagined them.

She knew it.

They'd reached her lodge. He was looking at her, waiting for her to signal their parting company. All she had to do was say a quick good-night and turn away. She had her key card in her purse.

But it didn't happen. Instead, she stayed where she was, gaze fixed on those dark eyes that were looking down at her. They looked *so* dark out here in the night. Pirate eyes. Eyes that tempted a woman to recklessness—wild dancing or lavish words or a thoughtless tumbling into bed.

And Lannie liked to be reckless, from time to time. How else could you find out what you wanted, when so much else hemmed you in?

"Um..." she said, and then her hand was reaching for him, for his cheek, a soft brushing caress that said *I want you* and *It's your turn now* in one simple movement.

She knew he wanted her. Knew it. Knew it utterly, in this moment, through some intuition of skin and heart that she didn't have a name for. Knew it in the way his face had gone still, his mouth firm and quiet, his jaw strong.

He closed his fingers around her wrist, still looking at her, not moving his gaze from her face. "Lannie..." he said. Her arm hung by her side now, with his long, lean fingers still making their warm bracelet against her skin, intensely comforting and intensely sensitizing at the same time.

She dropped her gaze to his lips, waiting for him to kiss her, just as a way of saying *Yes, I'm feeling it, too.*

Nothing more than that.

Not tonight.

She wasn't asking for more tonight. But she did want that one simple thing, the acknowledgment, the sense of a shared *yes*. It would feel…right. They were standing so close. And what a gorgeous mouth he had, a deceptively serious mouth that denied the heat and vitality in his eyes. Those lips were parting…

"Good night, Lannie. Enjoy your day off."

He'd let her go. She blinked stupidly, not believing it at first, not understanding that he was saying no. The way he might have encouraged a shy child to greet a new teacher, he turned her gently around and gave a light push against her back.

"Go on. You're tired. Got your key card? I'll wait while you find it."

She fumbled in her purse, too shocked and astonished and knocked off course for anything but obedience. She'd been *sure*…

But, yes, find the key, unlock the door, disappear inside, obediently and as quickly as she could, because she'd touched him and the only reason he'd touched her back was to push her away. "Thanks, yes. It's here," she said, the words feeling clumsy in her mouth.

When was the last time she'd been this gauche? When was the last time a man had rejected her like this? Oh shoot, and when had she ever felt compelled to make the first move, in any case? Recklessness was one thing, but this was a form of it that she'd never needed.

Her key card found the lock and swiped it open. She managed to stammer out the semblance of an acceptable goodnight and shut the door behind her so fast it would have slammed him in the nose if by some unlikely miracle he'd changed his mind.

He hadn't, though. She could hear him walking away. She actually peered through the security peephole to watch him, to see if he turned back with an expression of regret. Or any expression at all. Something that would tell her—

No. He'd reached the rose garden and was threading his way between the scented blooms.

No second thoughts, no hesitation.

Just as she was about to stop watching, however, he came to a halt and stood there for a moment, head bowed and fists clenched as if in the grip of a spasm of horrible pain. Her heart lurched in instinctive empathy and she almost ran out to him. But then the lines of his body firmed again. He kept walking, a silhouette against the night lighting at the hotel entrance.

She turned away from the peephole and said to herself through clenched teeth, "Atlanta Sheridan, get a grip!"

Sheesh, it was such a little thing. She'd made a tiny gesture of betraying need—not even need, just a simple question for him to answer—and he'd turned her away. No biggie.

And yet it burned because she didn't understand it. Didn't understand herself in making it or him in staying so firm.

She took a deep breath and reminded herself who she was.

Her father's only child.

Privileged.

Entitled.

Some people might say spoiled, but at heart she thought they were wrong.

Still, if she wanted, she could drop out of the Sheridan Lakes management role tomorrow and there'd be no consequences. Dad would be a little disappointed, but she'd quickly talk him round. He'd find her something else in a matter of days.

She didn't have to deal with a man who wanted her but wouldn't act on it.

She didn't have to deal with awkwardness in the work environment because she and a colleague couldn't find the right level.

Nope. It was easy. She could bail, the way she bailed out

of nightclubs when she was bored with the clientele, the way she'd once bailed out of a hiking trek in South America after the first two weeks because the combination of hairy spiders, a major stomach upset and a would-be boyfriend who was slow to take a hint took all the joy out of thick woollen socks and cool mountain air.

It should have been a comforting idea, that she could bail, but somehow it wasn't.

When she thought of it, all she could see was Nathan Ridgeway's face, with the closed, stoic expression he frequently wore.

He couldn't bail out, she knew. He didn't. He wouldn't. Not if it killed him. She somehow understood that in the whole course of his life, he never had.

It was a fundamental difference between them, and suddenly it fired her up inside. Intentionally or not, he wasn't going to defeat her. Not this fast. Not with something as tiny as taking her hand away when she touched his face.

Chapter Five

August, San Diego

"How exactly do you think I'd plan to bail out of something like this?" Lannie asked tightly.

"There are ways. Legal ways. Expensive ways." Nate spoke out of a blind anger and dread that had a whole raft of sources, most of which had nothing to do with Lannie herself. And yet the words came out anyway, as if banked in there for years. He was beyond operating on logic and fairness. "Ways for poor people, too, although I guess those don't concern you."

"Why do you think I'd want to? You're so sure of it. That really—"

"Because it's pretty much a habit with you, isn't it, as soon as you start to get in too deep, or something about the situation gets too hard?"

"Is this really the time to be *accusing* me?" She looked

white and sick, and he hated himself for it, realizing just how cruel he'd been.

"No," he said on a harsh whisper. "No, it's not. I'm sorry."

"You're sorry, but you said it."

"You have given me reasons, don't you think?" He tried to speak gently, this time, to point out that he did have some kind of a case, even if it wasn't a very good one, even if his timing royally sucked.

"Not in a situation like this," she bit back, her voice tight and rising. "I've had no time to think, to work out what I feel. I haven't even taken a pregnancy test to know for sure, and you're just hitting me with all these angry, negative predictions. Oh…oh…" She scrambled to her feet, suddenly, bending over her troubled stomach and heading for the bathroom. The door closed hard behind her, shutting him out.

He knew he deserved it, and he didn't dare to go knock and demand to be allowed to help her.

But at least their distance and separation gave them both a chance to think.

He picked up the phone and touched Room Service, getting a response after just one ring. "I need, let's see, dry crackers and cheese, and a platter of fruit, and hot tea. What kind? I don't know, some regular and some herbal, please. And can you make it fast? My—" His what? What was Lannie to him? What did she consider herself to be? "—girlfriend isn't feeling well, and really needs something to settle her stomach. Thanks. That's great."

He paced the luxurious room, waiting, thinking, sweating. Should he have tried to fake a reaction, just now?

Honey, a baby? That's wonderful! This is the best day of our lives.

His spirit rebelled.

It wasn't wonderful. Not yet. Not with the way things stood

between them. And with something as important and poten-
tially life-changing as this, wouldn't dishonesty and pretense
be the very worst way to start?

She didn't think it was wonderful, either. She'd said so,
before she'd even told him what the problem was. She'd said
she was scared, that she wasn't ready, and those were the
words that had triggered his accusations.

Still…

He should have held back. There was a middle ground.
Dishonesty and accusation hadn't been his only choices. Why
did he find it so hard to shake off the legacy of his childhood
and his family?

Because I'm still in the middle of it all.

No excuse. He wouldn't allow it to be an excuse. He'd
never hidden behind excuses in his life. He'd never shirked
his responsibilities, or let anyone down, and he wouldn't
start now.

He heard the rattle of the room service cart in the corridor
outside. The faucets were running in the bathroom again, and
he ached to do more for Lannie than this, but at least it was a
start. When the cart had been wheeled inside, he knocked at
the bathroom door.

"Lannie? Might it help if you eat something? I ordered
a couple of things, some fruit and cheese and crackers, and
they're here waiting as soon as you're ready. Or drink some
tea?"

He heard a muffled "Thanks. If there's chamomile tea,
could you make me some?"

"Yes, of course. Is there anything else? Tylenol or ice or
something? Do you want me to turn back the bed so you can
rest?" They were such little things, meaningless gestures of
care. If he could have solved this with action, he would have
climbed Mount Everest before nightfall.

"Just the tea."

"I'm sorry," he said again, even though it didn't help either of them, might actually make things worse.

"So am I," she answered through the door, and there were too many possible meanings behind the words.

Chapter Six

June, Upstate New York

"I goofed, Nate."

He turned to find Lannie several paces behind him in the light-filled walkway leading up from the pool to the main public areas of the hotel, and stopped to wait for her. "Housekeeping problem?"

She must have come from that department, while he was heading back from his twice-weekly survey of the grounds. She was carrying a plastic folder with a thin sheaf of papers inside. It seemed to him that she was always carrying something—a briefcase, menu folders, information binders, brochures from the hotel spa.

They were like theatrical props, or something. No, more like emotional shields. Weapons. Or camouflage. Proof, maybe, that she was taking her role seriously.

She didn't need them. She was taking her role seriously,

and he could see it. She'd been working incredibly hard at understanding the inner workings of the hotel, and all he'd heard about her from his staff was praise. She acknowledged any mistakes she made, she listened to the advice of others, she voiced her appreciation when she was given help. He wanted to tell her sometimes, "Relax! You've proved yourself. You don't have to try so hard," but when it came to the point, he didn't dare.

Because she was the boss's daughter, he told himself.

And knew he was lying.

It was that other thing that was the problem.

The thing in the air.

The attraction between them.

Three weeks ago, when it had almost come to something, he had said no in answer to her un-worded question and had turned away. He only hoped she had no idea what it had cost him, then and since, to keep his distance. If she'd sensed the struggle going on inside him, between good judgment on the one hand, and wild sensual need on the other...

Good judgment had won that night, but only just, and if she suspected how easily he could have gone the other way, it made him far too vulnerable. Maybe he needed her camouflaging binders and brochures even more than she did.

"No, nothing like that," she was saying, in answer to his question. She made a face, as they fell into step side by side. Typical, he thought, that she had greeted him with an announcement of her own failure—smiling at him, wryly apologetic and totally up-front. And what was with today's particular set of shielding paperwork? Had the workings of hotel housekeeping been interesting enough to generate that many notes, in the space of a couple of hours?

She messed with his head.

Daily.

Hourly.

The Atlanta Sheridan packaging and what lay beneath it seemed so much at odds with each other, he felt off balance every time he saw her, every time they exchanged a word or an in-house phone call or a conversation in short-hand gestures across the crowded main ballroom during an evening function.

She was cheerful and hardworking, honest and tactful, energetic and perfectly groomed. She liked wilderness hikes and Manhattan day spas, London nightclubs and sunsets in the mountains. She made his gut churn and his knees melt and his thought processes unravel, and if he'd won the struggle for good sense three weeks ago, he knew it wasn't a victory that was likely to last.

Especially if she guessed.

"It wasn't a big deal, really," she said, "but it got me thinking."

"Yeah?"

"A party of guests wanted some recommendations for hiking. It's about the tenth time I've been asked about this since I started here."

"While you've been at the concierge desk?"

"That's right." This was one of the training tools she'd insisted on, in the time she'd been at Sheridan Lakes. So far, as well as working at the concierge desk, she'd taken stints in the restaurant kitchens, the bar, the check-in, almost everywhere, at different times of day and evening, getting her hands dirty with ground maintenance, asking questions about the laundry service.

"It's not a surprise that people ask, is it? The Adirondack region has some of the best wilderness hiking in the country."

"Exactly! And these guys seemed pretty fit and keen so I told them about the Mount Panorama trail. They thought it sounded great, wanted to know the length and level of difficulty, I said it would take about four hours, with moderate

gradients and a well-marked route. Turns out I was a little…
uh…out in my estimates." She threw him a sideways smile
as they walked, like the casual toss of a tennis ball to a willing puppy, and he wanted to tell her, as he always did, *Stop,
Lannie*.

Stop making me want to be your best friend and your love
slave every time you look at me. Stop being so easy to work
with, so *not* the Daddy's-girl spoiled-heiress brat I thought I
could handle so cleverly, when I saw you at the airport.

"Or else I'm fitter than I thought," she went on, after the
smile. "I did that trail in less than four hours last summer, but
it took these guys more than seven. Taking a wrong turning
at one point despite the trail markers didn't help. They didn't
get back until nine-thirty last night and they were—well, you
can guess. Ticked off."

"How ticked off?"

"We worked through it."

"I mean, lawsuit ticked off? Free night's accommoda-
tion?"

"I told them a Lavande dinner was on the house, and they
were happy with that."

"Sounds like you did the right thing. So what did it get you
thinking about?" They came up a flight of steps to lobby level.
The hotel sloped down to the water, following the contours
of the land, and this was one of Nate's favorite ways of getting from point A to point B. The morning sun shone across
the lake and in through the wall of glass, giving light to the
artworks along the opposite wall. The long corridor doubled
as a gallery space, with changing exhibits by local artists,
available for purchase.

"It made me realize that Sheridan Lakes should be offering
more in that area," Lannie said. "I've been thinking about it
all morning in the housekeeping office." She flourished the

folder of papers. "I printed off a few ideas, during a spare moment."

"There's only so much excitement to be found in towel supplies and little bottles of shampoo, right?"

"Actually, I want to propose that we change our brand of shampoo, but that's a whole other subject." Another grin said that she knew he might consider her a pain in the butt, micromanaging the shampoo, but she was prepared to wear it. "Here's the thing. No one else on the concierge desk really knows about wilderness trips. All they can offer is the brochures for the various local rafting or trail-riding outfits, or suggest a visit to one of the Adirondack information centers."

"You don't think that's enough?" He probed his own instinctive reluctance and realized there was possessiveness involved. He loved hiking these mountains, himself. It was his favorite form of downtime, one of the few he allowed himself. Did he really want to share his beloved wilderness trails with hotel clients?

"No, I don't think it's enough. Not with the level of interest I've seen," she answered, using the crisp, professional tone that was so at odds with her full, kissable mouth. As always, the contradiction slugged him right where it hurt.

Focus, Nate. Of course you want clients to hike the trails if it keeps up the occupancy rate.

"I'm getting to be the go-to gal on the subject, now," Lannie was saying. "Which isn't going to work once I'm fully up to speed with higher-level management and less available for hands-on."

"No, you're right."

"As it stands now, whoever is working the desk calls me up for my expertise, and as we've just seen, that's not particularly accurate or reliable, because it's based purely on the hiking I've done here for years, not on an organized understanding of everything that's out there. It's barely an improvement on handing out brochures. We're just not giving the Sheridan level of service with this."

"So what are you suggesting?"

Keep talking, Lannie, because I just like to hear your voice. Only problem right now is that we're walking side by side, so I can't watch your mouth at the same time.

"As well as risking client dissatisfaction, I think we're missing an opportunity."

Yeah, missed opportunities, tell me about those. If I'd responded when you reached out and touched me that night...

"We should put together some hiking packages ourselves."

Hiking packages. Once more, he disciplined his thoughts, one kind of iron masculinity winning out over another. "How would that work?"

"Fully escorted by qualified guides with local knowledge, gourmet picnic hampers provided by the hotel kitchens, or sometimes lunch stops at quality regional restaurants, access to trails that can only be reached by boat or even helicopter drop."

"Wow."

"In other words, a unique, upmarket wilderness experience that's in keeping with the exclusive nature of a luxury Sheridan hotel and the vacation goals of our clients. Not everyone just wants to lie by the pool or sit in the bar, but they don't want to hike the trails that have half a million other tourists on them every day. They want to know that they're getting a special experience, and with a little work and research, we could—"

"Mr. Ridgeway?"

"Nathan, would you be able to—?"

"Oh, good, there he is..."

They'd reached the lobby. Three voices came at him at

once, from three different directions. "Lannie," he began, reluctance coloring his tone.

"You don't have time for my bright ideas right now," she guessed.

"No, I don't. But I'd really like—"

"Nathan, I'm sorry, it's pretty urgent..." interrupted one of his senior staff, looking harassed.

"I'm there," he promised, already starting to move in the direction of the main suite of managerial offices.

"Later," Lannie said. "If you think it's worth looking at any further."

"Yes. Definitely." He squeezed her hand, and then wished he hadn't. He had time to see the way she dropped her gaze at the moment of contact, saw the dent in her upper lip, and her blue eyes hooded by creamy lids and thick lashes, and wanted to step closer instead of moving away, heard himself say quickly, "How about dinner. Talk about it then? It's a quiet night. Seven?"

"Here?"

"No, not here," something made him say, although they could easily have taken a quiet corner in the bar. "Let's meet in the lobby, and we'll go to a place I know along the lake. Pretty casual. Don't dress up."

"It sounds great." She smiled at him one last time—what was it about her mouth?—and turned in the direction of the concierge desk and as always he didn't want to see her go, wanted to find any excuse to keep talking.

Here, Lannie, check these budget figures, propose your revisions to the fall menu, tell me what exactly is wrong with our current brand of shampoo. Can we order in the one you use on your own hair, because it looks like spun gold.

He listened to the latest crisis with their produce supplier with half his attention and kept the rest, helplessly, on the retreating figure of Lannie. The sound of her walk across the marble floor. The sound of her voice as she greeted a guest. The gleaming wheat-gold swing of that lustrous, beautiful hair, glimpsed at the very edge of his vision.

He'd been in trouble from the beginning with this woman. It wasn't going away, it was getting stronger day by day, and he'd just made everything harder for himself by transforming a business meeting into a dinner date.

And the worst thing about it?

He wasn't sorry, and he couldn't wait.

He wouldn't be sorry, Lannie vowed to herself.

Having had punctuality drummed into her as a vital courtesy from an early age, she was waiting for him at three minutes before seven, and he arrived in the lobby a minute after that. For the past seven hours she'd been expecting his voice on her cell phone, suggesting a change of plan. She'd imagined exactly how it would unfold.

On second thoughts—he would give a tactful clearing of the throat—he didn't think the wilderness packages would fly, under the Sheridan Lakes brand. Dinner wasn't necessary, he would say, and then promise her a ten-minute meeting in his office to try to sell the idea a little further, and if she couldn't convince him in that time, then of course she could go ahead with it if she wanted—she was the decision-maker, after all—but in his own opinion, they should let it go.

But no, the call didn't come, he didn't revise the arrangement, and here he was, and so was she, and she suddenly felt…

Nervous.

Girly and shy and expectant, as if this really was a date. First-kiss territory. Like prom night or New Year's Eve.

Which was stupid, because they'd had so many first date and prom night equivalents already, the shine should surely have worn off. There'd been that amazing wedding three weeks ago and at least fifteen significant hotel events since then, all of them with a party atmosphere and elegant dress and the glitter of good food and wine, music and beautiful lighting, and he'd made it very clear that nothing was going to happen.

So why tonight…?

But no, this *was* different.

They'd both dressed down for the occasion. Jeans and freshly washed hair. His had begun to grow out a little from the close-cropped cut he'd worn the day they'd met. He carried a leather jacket and smelled soapy and clean. She'd chosen a white lace and knit top with a scooped neck that didn't dip too low, a plain gold bangle, and heels she could actually walk in, because the need for Manolo-type therapy had worn off with the healing effect of the mountains.

"I'm glad you suggested getting away from the hotel," she said on an impulse, as they left the lobby together.

"Me, too. Sometimes a place like this can get to be your whole world, which some people might think helps me do my job better, but actually it doesn't."

"No?"

They walked in the direction of his car, parked in a small lot reserved for senior staff. He could have had the vehicle valeted to the front entrance, but she was glad he hadn't. No one had seen them leave. The lobby staff had been busy with clients, and their exit could have meant simply a routine survey of the hotel grounds or an admin errand. This felt private, casual, relaxed.

"The balance gets lost," he said. "The perspective."

They drove south along the lakefront and turned down a winding driveway to a cluster of resort cabins called Paradise Point. Right on the water beyond the cabins, set amongst the trees, there was a building that looked like an old-style

Adirondack mountain lodge, made of varnished wood and river stone.

"So how do you find the balance?" she asked him as they walked toward it from a parking area surrounded by tall pines. They hadn't said much to each other in the car, but she'd been thinking about what he'd said. Balance. Perspective. When you'd grown up with money, the way she had, those things could get lost in superficialities. It was something she tried hard to get right. She really didn't think she wanted a high-powered corporate lifestyle, long-term. So what was the answer instead?

"Well, I think you just have to schedule it in," he said. "For you, don't always use the hotel hair salon, for a start."

"I mean you personally. How do *you* find it?"

He answered her on a drawl. "How do I find the balance? I hike the mountains."

"You hike the—!" She realized the implications at once. "You never said, this morning."

"We were interrupted in the lobby."

"You never said three weeks ago, when I told you about hiking in Turkey."

"Our experiences don't match, Lannie. I've never hiked in another country, let alone been threatened with a kidnapping. These mountains are the only ones I know."

"So how come the concierge staff don't come to you for suggestions for hiking clients?"

"Because part of the balance is staying quiet about how I spend my free time."

"Yeah? You can manage that? In your big clumpy hiking boots? One thing I love about the footwear, so subtle."

"I head out early, pack my own food. I'm usually on a trail by six, when the sun is still low and the dew is on the ground. I'm sitting on a rock somewhere eating breakfast by eight, with no human habitation in sight, drinking thermos coffee and eating Danish. That's when you'll see bear and deer and mountain lion, if you're lucky."

"A mountain lion! I've only ever seen one, in all the summers I've been coming here."

"I've seen a few. But you're right that they're rare, even when you know where to look. On the way back, there's a swimming hole I like, on the Kushaqua River, very quiet, never anyone there. I strip off and take a dip. I keep a towel and a change of clothes in the car. Usually get back to the hotel around three, with the feel of the river water still on my skin, in time to deal with whatever has hit the fan since I left."

"Can I please take that tour?"

He laughed. "No package deals on that one. Strictly private, by special arrangement with the management. Especially the swimming part."

Suddenly, she could see it in her head—the two of them, lazy and near-naked in the water, washing away the heat and dirt of a day-long hike in the pristine mountain-river water. The picture almost made her gasp.

Actually had made her gasp, she realized, or else she'd given some other kind of perceptible reaction because he touched her back as if to steady her, and that one touch was all it took. She leaned in closer and tucked her arm around his waist before she even thought about it. She felt his cheek against her hair and the press of his chest against her side as he took a long, unsteady breath. He couldn't let her go. A part of him wanted to, but he couldn't. She could feel the warring emotions inside him, feel the burn of his need matching her own.

"Why won't you kiss me?" she blurted out.

"Because I like my job."

"This has nothing to do with your job!"

"You can't really think that, Atlanta." For once, he used

her full name. "You cannot possibly think that!" He stopped, turned her to face him, but didn't let her go.

Maybe he didn't realize that he was holding her, though, or *how* he was holding her. He ran his hands down her arms, anchored them on her hips, lifted them to softly touch her neck, wrapped his arms around her back, gestures of impatience and wanting that came direct from his dreams and unspoken desires. She knew, because she felt exactly the same.

"I do think that," she said. "It's just a job. There are options. Choices. *Parachutes.*"

"Parachutes?"

"Ways out. Dad can send me somewhere else if we do this—" They both knew what *this* was. "And then it doesn't work out, and we get to a point where we can't look at each other anymore."

"Send you somewhere else?"

"In a heartbeat. Sheridan Turfside, Sheridan Central Park. Or send you somewhere else."

"I don't want to go anywhere else. I came to these mountains twelve years ago to tend bar for the summer, and there's a reason I never left. I worked at six different places between Albany and Lake Champlain before I started at Sheridan Lakes, and my very first day there, I knew I'd come home."

"Me, then. I'll leave. This is not—"

He didn't wait to hear what it wasn't. "What is it, then? If you're so sure about what it's not, then tell me what it is."

"You know. You *know.* A first step. A really open, optimistic, positive first step. There have to be first steps. With everything. And you don't have to know what's at journey's end when you take them, or wouldn't we all still just be hovering right at the start line? Nate, you're not the kind of person who's scared of this stuff, are you? You don't strike me as someone who's scared of anything."

He didn't answer. His body had hardened against her.

Rebellion or strength or fear, she didn't know. She just knew it was powerful and he was in the grip of it and didn't have words.

Ah, but he didn't need words!

"Nate..." She whispered his name, feeling its importance on her lips, not trying to hide anything of what she felt. Confident, tonight, in a way she hadn't been three weeks ago when she'd reached up to touch his face.

He muttered something. Probably curse words. She didn't care. His hands were still on her neck, threading up into her hair. His mouth was only inches away, his breath a whisper of minty coolness on her lower lip. She waited, just waited, feeling her body fill with heat and hope.

More than hope.

Total belief.

Belief in the meaning of first steps, and especially *this* first step.

This kiss.

This man.

This mouth.

They were *right,* in a way she'd never felt before.

He brushed his lips against hers, seeking the contact and the bliss. His mouth was firm and sure and so...so personal. So giving and involved and instantly swept away. He kissed her as if she was the only woman in the world, as if they were the inventors of kissing, as if kissing was going to save the whole planet.

And she kissed him back. Wound her arms around him and pressed her body into his and tilted her face upward because he was so much taller and just gave herself to it, to the perfection and rightness of it that she'd known all along would be there.

It seemed like hours before they both slowly pulled away.

Lannie's mouth tingled and her whole body ached for more.

Nate had his hands on her hips, his weight heavy and unsteady as if he might need to lean on her for support. He looked at her with those dark, fathomless eyes, seeming helpless and unable to speak and she so didn't want him to say it—to say *anything,* right now, but especially not that he was sorry, or that they had to get ground rules in place, that they could be *friends with benefits,* or any of that halfhearted, bet-hedging, uncommitted stuff that so many of her friends seemed comfortable with, but that to her always felt so lacking in courage and fire and self-belief. She liked bold moves, strong choices.

"Don't say this was a mistake, Nate." It came out almost fiercely. "Don't you dare say that!"

"Uh… No. Okay."

"Were you going to?"

"I was going to kiss you again. When I'd made sure we could both breathe."

"Oh. Right."

"Can I do that?" He ran his fingers through her hair, then cupped the back of her neck, his hand warm and light.

"Yes."

"Good." Once more their mouths melted together, making discoveries, giving and demanding, tasting each other, teasing each other, slowing into stillness.

"Hell," he whispered, as if it was a kiss that had rocked his whole world. He was almost trembling, a man's kind of trembling, the kind that came from muscles bunched tight and strength that had nowhere else to go. He let out a sound that was half laughter, half a deep ragged sigh. "Hell! I knew it would be like this."

"Me, too."

"Yeah? Is that why the clipboards protecting your chest?"

"Multiple uses, those clipboards. I didn't want you to think—"

"What, Lannie?"

"That I was going to be...*difficult*."

"You haven't been difficult. You've been amazing. You just are...amazing."

It didn't make sense. Such a huge sense of shock, knocked sideways, both of them, by the power of how this felt. But *unsurprised* at the same time. How could that happen? How could those two polar opposite reactions exist together?

"We'd better go eat," he said. His intention seemed vague, and he didn't move.

"Yes," she agreed, and didn't move, either.

They'd been lucky so far. The private road giving access to the Paradise Point restaurant and cabins was quiet and the trees that screened the cabins from each other gave another kind of privacy, as well, but at any moment someone could come in or out, arriving to eat at the restaurant or leaving one of the cabins for an errand in town.

Lannie realized how much she would hate that—to have to pull apart like two teenagers on a front porch, because they'd been caught out. She didn't want to sneak around. She wanted to shout this to the mountain-tops.

"We'd better..." Nate began. "Get sensible, or something. For tonight, anyhow."

"How sensible?"

"Ah, not very. Just enough to— Hell, I so want to just—"

Take you to bed.

She didn't need him to say it out loud.

"We'd better eat," he concluded again, as if he meant it this time.

Then he kissed her again, a different kiss this time, joyful and exuberant and rough, a big smacking smooch on her mouth, squeezing her tight so she had to beg, while laughing, for breath.

She felt so expectant and happy and full of promise, as

if they'd both just taken the first step into paradise, the first step down a golden, magical road full of twists and turns that enticed and beckoned at every bend. Who knew where it would lead? Who knew where it would end?

Right now, those questions didn't matter. What mattered was the pleasure of the journey.

Chapter Seven

All his instincts and his experience told Nate that, even though he'd given into it, even though every cell in his body was singing with triumph, this wasn't going to be nearly as simple as Lannie seemed to think.

Nothing ever was.

It was the mistake his mother and sister made all the time, and they never, ever learned. Every fresh plan was always a glorious new dawn. Every possibility became a certainty in their expectations of the future. Every inevitable setback and failure came at them out of the blue, utterly unforeseen by either of them, even though Nate could have predicted it—and usually already had—from three thousand miles away.

But for Lannie tonight, what the two of them felt was utterly simple and perfect and reasonable, and he didn't have the will or the strength to tell her she was wrong. All through the meal she treated him like a lover, touching him, smiling into his eyes, laughing when he said something funny, nodding intently when he told her a couple of stories from his past, and he was so completely smitten that it terrified him inside. He couldn't even think of putting any more barriers in place, for his own protection or hers.

They talked about ideas for the wilderness hiking packages, didn't write anything down but he knew he'd remember every detail, because it was so tied up with her and their night, her voice, her enthusiasm, her quick mind. He told her to go for it, and said, yes, next week he'd off-load his other commitments, and hers, and spend a full day or even two taking her all over the mountains looking at the best trails, checking out the menus and ambience of possible meal destinations.

If they were going to do this, he agreed they should try to have a pilot version in place before the end of the summer, so they could assess it and have a full program up and running by next spring.

They talked about the jobs he'd had in his late teens before coming to upstate New York. Washing and moving second-hand cars at a low-rent dealership in L.A. Hotel porter at a thousand-room place near Disneyland. Lannie listened without judgment, didn't make any obvious comments about his struggle-street background. "A thousand rooms," she commented. "That would have been a learning curve, even in an entry-level job."

"I enjoyed it, too. Always something different going on. Seeing people at their best and their worst."

"Just the way it is with weddings."

"Yup, weddings are the same."

He didn't tell her exactly why he'd left California and come so far—another bad boyfriend of his mother's. Nate had tried to show Mom what the guy was really like but she wouldn't listen. She'd told him to pack his things and leave, and he had.

The rift had only lasted a couple of weeks—the bad

boyfriend lasted several months longer—but by the time he called home to find his mother willing to speak to him, he'd started at the bar up here and he didn't want to go back, even when Mom begged him to. He'd already understood that the physical distance between himself and his family might be the only thing that would save him and give him a future he could bear.

He asked Lannie about the rumor that she'd started a clothing line and it had folded.

"Never got as far as folding," she said. "I was looking into it for a while—an active women's clothing and footwear range—like, you shouldn't have to hike in brown boots—but there were other people pushing into that market, and I decided my timing was off and my commitment wasn't as there as it needed to be."

"The rumor had it wrong, then."

"What did the rumor say?"

"Lingerie, not hiking boots."

"I'm a hotel heiress. Of course they're going to assume it would be lingerie. Messing with stereotypes is one of my favorite hobbies."

"Let me tell you, you do it really well!"

She laughed, then sighed. "I wish my parents agreed with you."

"I'm lost," he kept thinking. "I'm lost... What the hell am I going to do? Where the hell is this going to lead? This is magical...and I can't let myself trust it. I can't!"

He barely tasted the food or the wine. Knew in the back of his mind that they were delicious...simple...perfect for the occasion...but they weren't important. He barely heard the ambient music or the growing noise of the other diners. They'd been given the best table—he knew the owner—at the outer corner of the deck which almost seemed to jut over the water, and for a long time this gave them a sense of seclusion and privacy.

Eventually, however, the place filled up, one or two groups of diners had ordered more drinks than they probably should have, and the sense of intimacy slipped away. At the next table, two of the men began a mock fight, roughed each other up across the table and then swapped a couple of crude jokes. One of them bumped the back of Lannie's chair quite hard.

"Want to change seats?" Nate offered quietly.

She shook her head.

"They'll settle down. Their wives just exchanged a look that meant business."

"Let's leave," she said, and he heard her father's quick decisiveness in her voice. "This isn't fun anymore."

"You just ordered dessert."

"I'll ask for it to go, when we fix up the check." She'd already stood up.

The man who'd bumped her looked over his shoulder, a little startled to find how close her chair was. "I'm so sorry," he said, slurred but sincere. "Was that your chair?"

"Yes, it was."

"Look, I'm sorry."

"No problem." She delivered a beaming, golden smile but stayed on her feet, sliding gracefully between the crowded tables, her intent unwavering.

Nate followed, not quite sure what was happening. One accidental chair bump and she was out of here? Was the bump just an excuse? But if she'd been wanting to leave for a while, why the dessert? Her actions were so at odds with his mood of simple happiness, his head couldn't catch up.

She waited for the dessert at the front desk, her whole presence still radiant and beautiful but her spirit absent, somehow. She'd disengaged, he saw. The afterglow had switched off.

She took the wedge of raspberry frangipane tart in its

plastic box and they left the restaurant, stepping out into the cool and quiet of an Adirondack summer night. Yellow light glowed in the windows of the cabins. A group was playing half-court tennis in the dark, with a glow-in-the-dark ball. It bounced along as if it belonged in a karaoke machine marking time to the lyrics, then it escaped the court and landed at Nate's feet. He picked it up and threw it back. "Thanks, buddy," someone said.

"Would you like this?" Lannie offered him the frangipane tart.

"No, it's yours, and you could have eaten it in the restaurant. What happened?"

She shrugged. "Those guys weren't going to settle down. I didn't want to wait until they'd spoiled the whole mood."

It seemed to him that she was the one who'd spoiled the mood, pulling the plug so fast, not giving their evening a chance to bounce back. Nate had lost the afterglow, too, in the process. He wanted to stop her beside the car and kiss her again, but she wasn't giving off the right signals. He opened the passenger door for her and she slid inside, smiling at him and tilting her head, making him want her so much it hurt, but he didn't have the right script for this.

"Please take the cake," she said. "I don't want it anymore."

"Okay, I'll take the cake." He tossed the box into the backseat.

Leaving a restaurant this fast was what you did when you couldn't keep your hands off each other any longer. It was a *positive* thing, a huge step toward the future. He hadn't been planning or assuming that they'd end up in bed tonight, but he kind of thought the whole thing would be clearer at this point, that they'd have moved in a consistent direction.

Now, he wasn't sure.

The whole drive back he wasn't sure, but when he pulled

up outside her lodge, she turned to him and said, as if it was the most obvious, natural thing in the world, "Are you coming in?"

His pulses leaped beneath his skin, his heart went, "Yes!" and he almost pumped his fist in the air. And yet when they reached the steps up to her door, he put a hand on her shoulder and held her back. "Hey..."

"Mmm?" Her expression was smooth and untroubled.

"Tell me more about what happened back there, why we just had to leave."

"Those guys—"

"You don't know that they wouldn't have settled down. We could have shifted the table a little. Or just tuned them out. Moved upstairs to the bar. I don't know why they had to be a deal-breaker, when we were having such a great time."

She shrugged again. "I like to pick my battles, and this was such a little one, it didn't seem worth trying to win. It's not important, is it? We're here."

"Yes, and something is—" But he didn't know how to finish. He didn't know what was troubling him, what the *something* was. She'd given a reasonable explanation, and it made sense. What was that saying? Don't sweat the small stuff. None of it should be a major issue.

She stepped close and laced her fingers together behind his neck, looking up into his face, pressing her body gently against him. His groin throbbed with need, his head swam and his heart gave dizzy, uneven beats. "Can we forget it? Move on?"

Move on, and into bed.

Hell! When had he ever in his life turned down a woman he wanted this much! How long, in fact, since he had wanted a woman this much? Had he ever? "I'm sorry, Lannie," he said slowly. "This is good-night, I think."

"You really have a problem with the two of us standing

outside my lodge, don't you?" she said softly. "This happened before…"

"You could be forgiven for thinking that."

"So what is it?"

"Let's take it slow," he heard himself say. "Let's get to know each other a little more first, and not just around the hotel, when we're working."

"No?"

"You talked about first steps, before. How about we don't rush those? They're precious, aren't they?"

"Incredibly precious."

"They're important. You never get a second chance with them. You take them, and that's it, they're gone. Let's take them right."

"So this isn't *no,* it's just *not tonight.*"

"Of course it's not *no!*" She must be able to feel the effort this was costing him. *No* would kill him at this point. *Not tonight* was almost giving him a mortal wound.

"Because I couldn't handle those guys bruising our mood?"

"No… Okay, yes, a little. Don't push this."

"So do I get a kiss?"

"You get about a thousand kisses." Because he didn't dare to give her just one. A thousand was safer.

He kissed her hair and her temples and her forehead, her neck, the lobe of one ear, her jawline, the soft place below her cheekbone, the corner of her mouth. And there he stopped and eased away, because if he gave her that one real, full kiss on her mouth, filled with heat and generosity and male demand, there was no way he could turn around and climb back in his car tonight without taking her to bed first.

"Good night, Lannie."

"Can we at least decide on a day for taking the next step? Explore those trails and eating places?"

"Wednesday? And Thursday, if we need more time."

"Can't wait." She slipped inside her front door, smiling at him until it closed between them.

Three days, two weddings and a convention of golf-fanatic accountants later, he discovered the frangipane tart still in its plastic box on the car's backseat, the raspberries a fermenting mess and the tart itself curling and half dried out.

He tossed it in the trash, but it bothered him somehow.

The tart deserved better.

"So tell me how it's going, four weeks in," Lannie's father said.

"Well, that's something I want to talk to you about, actually." They were seated at the terrace bar, with the morning sun sparkling on the lake, and coffee hot and fresh in front of them. Dad had flown in this morning and his private helicopter still sat on the helipad on the far side of the Sheridan Lakes resort, ready to fly him out again this afternoon.

Lannie suspected that her mother was behind the unexpected visit. "Go check up on Lannie, Bill," Mom would have said. "She's been sounding a little flaky on the phone, the past few days. If I come she'll see right through us, but if we pretend you're there for the hotel…"

"Problems?" Dad asked.

"No, not at all. But I want to change the deal. Something else has come up."

"Something else? You're leaving, after just four weeks?" He looked disappointed, the same expression she remembered seeing on his face several times in recent years.

When she'd told him she wanted to travel for a couple of years before she took on a major role with Sheridan Hotels, for example. And when she'd dropped out of her MBA with less than a year to go. Most notably, at the age of twenty-two, when she'd broken off her engagement to the highly suitable Walton Milford III six weeks before their wedding.

"No, I'm not leaving," she told him quickly, so that his expression would change.

She hated disappointing him, and he never understood her reasons. He talked about "bailing" and she called it that herself, now, out of sheer stubbornness and frustration at how difficult it was to communicate to him who she was, how difficult it was to even know who she was when her parents recognized such a limited repertoire of options.

Should she really have gone ahead and married Walton, once she'd realized that all she was thinking about was the wedding, and not the actual marriage? Should she really have stalled another three or four weeks before she broke the news to everyone, to make sure it wasn't just bridal nerves? It wasn't nerves. Wasn't it better to bite the bullet on these things, get the announcement over with as soon as the decision was made? She'd inherited that very trait from Dad, hadn't she? He always liked to move quickly on his decision. And at least, six weeks out, they hadn't had a massive pile of gifts to return and an uneaten cake to waste.

And yet both her parents had projected their disappointment in various ways for a long time. Maybe they still were.

"So what's happening?" Dad said, still looking suspicious, ready to talk her round.

"I'm stepping back from the management role, that's all. I should never have taken it in the first place, Dad. You shouldn't have pushed Nathan Ridgeway aside."

"You sounded distraught on the phone from Turkey."

"That didn't mean you had to move instantly to a high-power solution. I've tried to fill the position in name only, leave all the important part of it to him, but that's underhand, somehow. I can't pretend to be learning the ropes forever."

"You're still not telling me about the something else."

"I'm getting to that." She outlined the wilderness packages and saw the disappointment again. He must have been hoping she'd decided to go back and finish her MBA.

Putting together a tour program just wasn't *big* enough for Dad. Working in a Thai orphanage hadn't been big enough, either. He would have preferred her to take on a high-profile promotional role—the celebrity face of the charitable foundation instead of one of its grassroots volunteers. He would have liked to see her pushing sponsorship and donations in TV campaigns, launching fundraising dinners, having her photo in the brochures, hugging a child.

He'd predicted she wouldn't last out the year in Thailand. Even Mom had made a little jab along the lines of, "If you can't stick out a Harvard MBA, how're you going to stick out poverty in Thailand?"

But she had "stuck it out."

Now she had to stick to her guns over the wilderness tours.

She talked her father through the idea a little more, to be rewarded by a statement that he just didn't understand *why.* Sure, it was a good proposal, he could see the commercial potential, and she was right, it would fit with the Sheridan branding if it was done in the right way, but why did she have to be the one to do it? Why not delegate? "It seems to me that you're dropping out of the management position on a whim."

"It's not a whim, Dad."

Problem was, she couldn't fully explain her reasons, because she couldn't talk about Nate.

Or rather, she could have talked about him in a heartbeat, if she'd had the right person on hand to listen. Her best friend Jane, for example, but Jane lived in London and cell phones just weren't the same as face-to-face.

If this had been Mom, she might have said more—some

girlie, indulgent heart-to-heart stuff about the spark she felt, the sense of promise. She *might*. Would Nate want that? But not to Dad. Dad liked to cut to the chase. The whole Walton experience had taught her that Dad didn't even want to hear the guy's name until they were ready to announce the engagement.

"Still, why you, honey?"

"Because it's an area of interest and strength for me. Because it gets Nate back where he belongs, in the top job, without either of us—or you, for that matter—losing face over the whole thing."

And because it makes it far less awkward for Nate and me to be personally involved, especially if it doesn't last…

Her father sighed, and shifted in his seat, both actions seeming a little petulant, and suddenly *older*. He was nearly sixty-five, and for the first time Lannie felt shocked about it, confronted by it. He wasn't going to live forever. He drove himself hard and didn't take care of his health the way he should. He was incredibly stubborn about changing his ways. "The *V* word"—vegetables—had been banned from her mother's lips, and even his doctor only dared speak of vitamin capsules and antacid medication when it came to Dad's diet. "I thought you'd decided to settle down, Lannie."

He wanted her to get married, she realized, and not just for the reasons of business and status which had lain behind his pleasure—and then his disappointment—over Walton. He wanted grandchildren. As an only child, it was up to her to provide, in that department.

"This is a kind of settling down," she told him gently. "Or it could be, if it works out. I've always loved it in these mountains. If I stay here, buy my own place, maybe, it'll be to do something I love. I don't necessarily need to head up the Sheridan Hotel Empire. There are shareholders and board members and managers for that. Don't push, Dad. Have some trust in my decision making. Let me find out for myself what I really want."

"Can I? Have that trust? After—"

Please, not Walton again, not the MBA…

"Try!" she cut in quickly. "Don't make me justify everything I do. And don't act as if my whole adult life has been lived on the rebound from one mistake to the other. Let me work out who I am, in my own way. Maybe I'm not cut out to be a corporate highflier like you." She reached across the table and chafed the back of his hand to soften the words, and he nodded.

"Just promise me you're thinking things through. Sometimes you seem to act too much on instinct and impulse, Lannie."

"I think my instincts are good."

"I'm not saying they aren't, but you need to back them up with a little patience and hard thinking, before you take action. Some directions in life are a one-way street. You can't just turn around and drive back the other way. Your mother and I…" He trailed off, as if the words he wanted to say were too personal and too emotional.

So she said them on his behalf. "Care about me. Worry about me. I know, Dad. I know how much I'm loved, and you shouldn't underestimate how much that gives me, how much direction I have in my life, what a powerful compass point, just purely from that."

"Good. Yes. I'll remember that." He seemed gruffer than ever, signalling clearly that the personal part of their conversation was over, and she realized he was looking over her shoulder at someone's approach. Bill Sheridan of Sheridan Hotels didn't want to get caught out by a member of his staff in a sentimental moment. He stood up and reached out his hand and it was Nate standing there, greeting him.

"Bill, good to see you."

"Nathan… Lannie and I have finished and she's just now given you and me a couple more things to discuss, so let's get started. Do you want coffee?"

Lannie recognized her dismissal from the scene. Nate met her eye and they both held the look for a fraction of a second too long. It had been four days since their kiss. Four very busy days, during which they'd agreed with just a few phrases to put a hold on what had begun, to give themselves a chance to cool off or rethink, for the moment, at least.

Lannie's thinking hadn't changed a thing, and she was sure that Nate's hadn't, either. On Wednesday they were spending the whole day together on their own, exploring the mountains. And then…how did that song go?

All night long…

Chapter Eight

Lannie stared at her reflection in the huge, gleaming mirror of the hotel bathroom. Her face was blotched with uneven color, her eyes swimming with tears, her hair like a haystack roughly tied with twine. She looked hunted and defeated and miserable.

All of that, and more.

She felt trapped in here, not ready to go out and face Nate yet, even though the lure of hot, soothing tea, dry crackers and cool, juicy grapes was strong.

He's right, she kept thinking.

It killed her that he'd said it so bluntly and with such cruel accusation, but the bottom line?

At some level, he was right.

All her habitual instincts were kicking in and she was looking for a way out, the way she'd found a way out of an MBA degree she didn't really want, and a marriage she'd known in her heart wouldn't last. She'd always believed that she'd done the right thing on both those occasions, but maybe she was wrong.

Maybe she should have stuck out the MBA just to prove she could, or married Walton in a big splashy wedding to save his dignity and opted for a quiet divorce when the fuss died down. Maybe she had too much of Dad's impatience when it came to acting on decisions. Maybe her hunger and impatience to find out who she was, outside of the obvious choices laid before her, had actually slowed down her quest for answers.

There'd been several lesser bailouts in her life, too, and Nate had witnessed one or two of them at first hand and drawn his own conclusions. Were those conclusions right?

This time, there was a life growing inside her, and the looming probability of the most important decisions and choices she would ever have to make.

A life…

She was almost certain of it. She hadn't connected the dots until this morning when the vague nausea of the past few difficult days suddenly coalesced into a stomach in full rebellion, but as soon as that happened, so much else made sense. The fact that everything smelled and tasted weird. The ever-increasing soreness in her breasts. Her period two weeks overdue, or even more. Thinking back, she wondered if those wisps of blood six weeks ago—and already late, then, too— had even been her period, or were they something else?

She'd put all of it down to the travel at first. Her cycle was often irregular. She'd travelled too much over the past few years to keep it tied to the moon the way nature intended. The weird sense of smell she had decided belonged to San Diego. The water was different here, and the food, the taste of the air. The kind of cheap bar food and on-the-run snacks she'd been eating with Nate's family weren't what she was used to, either.

She hadn't even had an inkling until this morning, which meant that when she did connect those telltale dots, she was totally unprepared.

There was a life growing inside her, which made the stakes so much higher.

She tried to make plans, to envisage the future, needing to reach some kind of understanding of her situation before she said another word to Nate.

If they could manage to speak to each other at all.

Okay, for a start, termination was out. She didn't even need to explore her reasons, the gut-level rejection of the idea came instinctively and with a powerful certainty. This little life didn't deserve her to bail out to that extent.

So, somewhere between six and seven months of pregnancy still lay ahead.

Doable. Let's stay practical about this, Atlanta Marie Sheridan, let's not overwhelm ourselves with detail and emotion and worst-case scenarios.

She was healthy, and she had good medical cover. Provided she ate well, took care of herself, went through all the right prenatal checkups and tests, the pregnancy itself shouldn't be too big of a deal.

But then…

A thousand questions danced a frenzy in her head.

Breathe, Lannie.

Don't panic.

There are nannies. There are summer camps and day-care programs. There's boarding school. You don't have to do this on your own, twenty-four-seven, even if you're on paper a single mom. You'll still be *you,* whoever you are. A baby doesn't have to change everything. Maybe it doesn't have to change very much at all.

But what about Nate? Wonderful, complicated, struggling Nate?

She could hear him in the other room. There were chinking sounds as he poured the chamomile tea, and the dull rumpling noise of bedding being folded back. In her absence, he was taking care of her with a tenderness he hadn't been able to show to her face, just now.

What exactly did you want him to say, Lannie?

At this, she drew a blank. What could he have said? That he'd be there for her until their child went off to college? Actions spoke louder than words, and she already had evidence that Nate took care of the people in his life far more than was healthy for his own well-being.

Did she want him to say that he thought they should get married?

Lord, they hadn't gotten that far! They'd be crazy to get married when there were major issues looming between them that weren't going to be easy to resolve. She'd been down that road with Walton and she'd escaped just in time. Sheesh, of course she shouldn't have gone ahead and married him!

Speaking of resolving things… It was time to leave the safety of the bathroom. She had to face Nate eventually. Best to get it over with. After a final attempt to deal with the ravages the nausea and emotion had made to her face and hair, she opened the door.

There he was, standing waiting for her, on full alert as soon as he'd heard her movement and the click of the door, his expression eager and suffering at the same time, his strong shoulders tight and his hands working at his sides. He reached out for her before she could speak or move and engulfed her in a huge, warm hug, tender and strong and delicious, so familiar now, so wanted always.

She couldn't speak, and all he said was her name. "Lannie…" A hot, suffering breath of sound against her hair. She nestled into him, burrowed into the warmth of his body like a newborn kitten, her limbs weak and shaky, and for one long, precious moment everything was all right.

Chapter Nine

July, Upstate New York

"**W**hat a great day!" Nate leaned against the back of the seat and looked at Lannie, seated behind the wheel.

They'd taken turns with the driving and his male ego had no problem with sitting back and watching her while her attention was fixed on the winding back roads. She had a profile like a Renaissance painting, hair like fairy-tale straw turned to gold, eyes like the clearest sapphires and a tan on her bare shoulders as smooth and brown and creamy as the foam on a double-shot espresso.

"You're saying that as if it's over," she answered, flashing him a quarter-second glance and then fixing her eyes back on the road. She was a confident driver, but always within the right limits.

"Okay," he corrected obediently. "What a great day *so far.*"

"Much better." She grinned, looking like a TV commercial for mountain spring water.

"You want to check out this final trail, or are you getting tired? Is it too late in the day?"

"Watch it, Ridgeway. Tired? I think I'm fitter than you are. We're only talking a few miles for this one, aren't we?"

They must have covered over twenty miles so far, on three different trails, starting almost at first light, and he was hugely impressed with her stamina and attitude. No complaints, no constant chatter. She saved her breath for the walking, and her appreciation came in the quiet contemplation of a view while they sat on a rock to take a break, or a long, thirsty pull on her bottle of ice-cold water, or a quick grab of his arm to point out an animal he hadn't seen in the dappling camouflage of the woodland light.

When he'd kissed her at nine-thirty in the morning, beside a rushing stream, she'd teased him with it, kissing him back with sweet, seductive promise before she pulled away, her lips softly parted and her voice sultry and low. "Later. We're here to work, remember?"

"Later?" Do you mean that, Lannie? When, later? Tonight? And what are you promising?

"If you want. You're the one who's been putting on the brakes," she'd reminded him gently. "Don't change the rules now."

"I haven't— It's not because—" Lord, she threw him sometimes! She was right, he *had* put on the brakes, but still he instinctively expected her to be the one playing hard to get. She *should* be the one. How come she couldn't apply a little caution? Did she honestly not perceive any risks to this at all? The way she threw herself into life almost scared him, for reasons he was still trying to work out.

"I know," she'd soothed him, saving him from the struggle to complete his words. "It's okay." She was still smiling. "It's because you're more cautious than I am, and...you know... maybe it's good that we're a little different that way. You think about consequences, and I sometimes don't. Life's too short."

"It isn't," he answered automatically.

His mother and sister said that to him all the time, to justify their crazy plans. *Life's too short to save up that kind of money. Life's too short to stay in a boring job if they're not going to see my potential for promotion up front. Life's too short not to go after my dream right now.*

But they were wrong.

Lannie was wrong.

"Life is long, actually, for most of us, if you think about it, especially when you mess it up," he told her. "Mess-ups can last for years. Forever. Debt and bad divorce and dangerous driving. It can affect your whole life, and the lives of your kids, and their kids."

"You think we'll mess up our whole lives for ever and ever, just by getting involved?"

Yeah, okay, it sounded melodramatic and ridiculous, put that way. And yet...

"I need to...uh...scope out that possibility in advance, just to be on the safe side."

She'd laughed at this, with the morning sun bright in her face and the whole world fresh and perfect, not even a cloud on the horizon, let alone a train-wrecked life. But then the laughter had stopped and she'd said seriously, "Yeah, okay. I respect that. I see the sense in it. You're a clever man, aren't you, Nate? And sensible. You're sensible."

Another thing his family said to him, making it sound like a character flaw. "Being sensible gets a bad rap that it doesn't deserve," he said, voice gruff, catching a little in his throat. "I don't call it being sensible, I just call it thinking things through."

"You mean, I wouldn't set out on a twenty mile hike without planning it, and packing water and food and emergency gear, so I shouldn't set out in a relationship without doing the same?"

"Something like that."

"What emergency gear do I need with you, Nate?"

"Oh, parachute, ice pick, defibrillator, just the usual. You can fit all of it in the side pocket of your day-pack."

Once again, she'd laughed.

After this, they hadn't talked for quite a while. He felt more attuned to her without conversation than he would have if they'd chattered back and forth the whole time, and he'd begun to have the dangerous belief that maybe she really was perfect, just completely perfect.

He wondered dazedly if this was really the same woman who had a regular date at the hotel spa and salon every week, who rarely seemed to wear the same outfit twice at the hotel's constant roster of glittering functions, and who had a bikini body—glimpsed by Nate not *totally* by accident during an early morning swim in the hotel pool—that would make most other women contemplate the immediate need for surgery and a three-month vegetable juice diet.

If the glamorous, pampered heiress had been the only side to Lannie's personality, she would have bored him in a week, but he had *noooo* problem whatsoever with the complicated and contradictory nature of her being. A bikini body *and* thigh muscles beneath those designer clothes? Salon hair *and* top-of-the-range lime-green hiking boots high on her priority list? Hot celebrity gossip *and* world events in her repertoire of conversation?

He was in so much trouble, letting her trespass this deep into his life this fast, and he didn't even care. He felt reckless and confident and as if nothing in his life could possibly fail.

Maybe there was more of his mother and sister in his character than he'd ever admitted to before…

"We have a dinner reservation at Moose Lake Lodge at eight," he reminded Lannie now. They needed to make a decision about hiking this final trail.

"We'll make it before dark," she predicted, confident. "Or almost. If we don't, I have an L.E.D. flashlight in my day-pack that'll blind a black bear at fifty paces. And I brought a change of clothes for going out. If they don't hold our reservation, we'll find somewhere else." As usual, she made a possible change of direction sound easy. Maybe he should adopt her philosophy more often. "Oh, is this the turning, coming up, that leads to the trailhead?"

"Yup, this one on the left."

A few minutes later she'd parked on the apron of gravel adjacent to the marked trail. It was almost seven in the evening by this time, and the light had begun to stretch and thin and deepen into gold. There were no other cars here at this hour, no indication of anyone camping overnight. They should have the trail to themselves, and they still had food and water, as well as waterproof jackets in the unlikely event of a sudden weather change.

Once again, it was a magical walk, through still, quiet woodland carpeted in soft leaves. The air smelled peaty and fresh, and they saw an eagle soaring overhead, and beaver dams reflecting the contours of the mountains. At the top of the trail they came to a high lake with a wooden lean-to looking out over the water. A ring of blackened stones, a barbecue fork hanging on a nail and several burned down citronella candles pointed to the fact that hikers camped here frequently, but they were lucky this evening. They were alone.

Totally alone.

Lord, that did crazy things to Nate's body!

He'd wanted Lannie all day, every time he watched her

peachy backside as she strode ahead of him on the trail, or when he turned to wait for her coming up behind him, and saw the sunlight in her golden blonde hair, the clean shimmer of sweat on her forehead, the long, tanned reach of her legs in her cutoff denim hiking shorts.

He'd wanted her, but he'd told himself to wait. They'd passed several other hikers on those earlier and better-known trails. There hadn't been anywhere near this sense of solitude and privacy. And he hadn't been thinking creatively. His fantasies had revolved around getting her into bed.

But maybe they didn't need an actual bed...

Ah, hell! Don't go there, Nate.

She sat on a rock, slid her day-pack from her shoulders and took out her water bottle and a foil-wrapped block of chocolate. "My feet are starting to get tired. I'm glad it's soft ground, and downhill on the return trip." She took a swig of the water, laid the wrapped chocolate on the rock and reached down to her boots, untying and loosening the laces with her pretty fingers, sliding off boots and socks. "Don't come too close until these puppies have cooled down a little, Nate!"

"Don't worry, I'll be sitting on my own rock, cooling a couple of puppies of my own."

Well, he would be once he'd finished watching her. She slid her feet into the cool water that lapped the rock and gave a moan of ecstasy as she wriggled and stretched her toes. "Ohh, that feels so good!"

He couldn't tear his eyes away, fumbling at his own laces without looking at them, taking five times as long to get his boots and socks off than if he hadn't had her as a delectable distraction. She dabbled her toes in the water, splashed her feet back and forth, reached down and massaged them beneath the water line, then slid her legs in up to her knees. "Would we be crazy to swim, Nate?"

"We'd be crazy to get our clothes wet, at this hour. They

wouldn't dry, and it'll chill later, and if something happened on the return trail and we had to spend the night out in the open in wet fabric, one of us with an injury…"

She made a face at him. "Being sensible again, Nathan Ridgeway?"

"Yeah, so shoot me, I like survival better than a hospital morgue. These mountains aren't just painted backdrops, and the trails aren't theme-park rides. Weren't you the one nearly killing yourself on a Turkish mountain a few weeks ago, because a risky situation came up that you hadn't foreseen?"

"Point taken," she said. "No swimming in our clothes," and sat back and picked up the chocolate instead.

It had melted a little in the heat of the day, and she had to peel the foil wrapping back carefully. Her fingers were so delicate, taking the chocolate squares and breaking them apart. Softened, they came easily, but melted at once with her body heat, before she could pop them in her mouth. "Mmm, I'm going to get in a mess, but I don't care."

Nate didn't care, either. She had a smear of chocolate on her lower lip and had to lick her thumb and finger clean. Did she really have no idea that he was so mesmerised by this? That he wanted to *be* those little squares of chocolate, disappearing into her mouth?

Huh.

Darn.

She'd caught him out.

Of course she had, since he was in too much of a state of voyeuristic bliss to hide it.

She lifted her sunglasses to the top of her head and smiled at him, a playful, wicked and newly aware smile. "Have I been putting on a show without knowing it?"

"Did you really not know it?"

"No, I didn't, not till just now. It was all about the feet and the chocolate and the water, until I saw you. I admit, I was having a few ideas about not getting our clothes wet and how we might achieve that and still get our swim."

"You saw me watching," he said.

"And then the chocolate stopped being important."

"It's still important to me..." he said. Gruffly. Because she hadn't yet licked it from her lower lip.

Misunderstanding—or maybe not—she scrambled to her feet and came over to his rock, holding out the foil like a silver platter. She knelt on the mossy grass beside him, took some chocolate and slipped it into his mouth, and he let it spread its sweet darkness over his tongue.

Not because he wanted it.

Just to keep her this close.

To keep her fingers soft against his lips, tasting of sugar. Helplessly, he let his eyes drift shut and his tongue play with her. When she began to take her hand away, he closed his fingers around her wrist and pressed chocolate kisses into her palm, and onto her knuckles and fingertips.

"Nate?"

"Mmm?" He opened his eyes, let go of her hand, mastered control of his mouth. He felt drunk on chocolate and the taste of Lannie.

"Is it...?" she began, looking at him with very serious blue eyes. Her voice was quiet, almost tentative and scared, suddenly. "I mean, is this—? Have you done your thinking, Nate? Your scoping out?" She leaned forward, placed a hand lightly on his bare knee.

"I can't have done enough of it, not this fast." He was issuing a warning to himself as much as to her.

"No?"

"But I've done all I have in me to do." Hell, he could hardly get the words out! His voice was like gravel. "I want you so much. If you want me, too..."

"Oh, I do. I do! Why do you keep thinking I'm going to

change my mind, when it's you who pulls back? Haven't I made it so, so obvious? I feel like a mountain lion stalking my kill. *Hunt* me a little bit, Nate. Do some of it for me. Do as much as you want."

"Right now?"

"Yes, now, please, now. I—I—You'll be proud of my planning skills, Nate. I brought a pack of condoms, right in the pocket of my shorts."

"So did I…"

"You did?" She laughed. "Isn't that perfect?"

Ah, hell! She still had that hand on his knee, so light and soft, not moving, nothing so obvious as a seductive caress, just resting there all shy and uncertain.

He leaned into her, precarious on the rock, and pulled her to her feet. Or else she pulled him. It wasn't clear. It didn't matter. They came together in a hot press, their arms and thighs meeting way before their lips. Her bare foot brushed his, all cool and firm and clean from the water. He brushed his mouth against her neck and faintly tasted salt and sunscreen and the citrusy smell of bug cream. She planted her hands against the backs of his thighs and his groin leaped in response.

"There's nobody here," she whispered.

"I know."

"But we'll be late for our dinner reservation."

"I don't care. Do you?"

"No." She pressed her whole length against him, those long, creamy-brown, athletic legs, her gym-toned stomach, her breasts the way nature made them, neat and high and just the right size for his hands, in a smooth T-shirt bra. Pale blue. Not that he'd taken note, or anything.

He kissed her and she still tasted of chocolate. He caught that smear from her lower lip at last and took it for himself, pushing down his greed for her because otherwise he would have gone too fast and too hard. She would have had her clothes off in fifteen seconds and he would have been wrenching and cursing at his. He couldn't let this unfold badly. They both deserved more than a messy rush.

"Lannie, Lannie…" He kept saying her name because her name slowed him down, kept his compass points in place.

"Yes?"

"Nothing. Just want to say it."

"Oh…" The sound of understanding sighed against his mouth and he kissed her as full and deep as he'd ever kissed a woman in his life. It went on and on, sweet and perfect, out in the open air with acres of sky and mountain and lake all around them yet so intensely private he felt as if his heart had burst right out of his chest.

The grass was soft and thick, and a steady breeze kept the mosquitoes at bay. He slid his hands beneath her T-shirt and she said, "Yes…" and helped him, lifting it over her head and dropping it on the grass. He worked at his own shirt with less patience and grace, and loved the way she reached out at once to run her hands over his chest.

It wasn't enough. She unhooked her bra and they closed together once more. Her bare, warm breasts pushed against him. He could feel their peaks already hard with need, but it was nothing to the way he was hard, straining at his shorts, throbbing and hurting with his urgency. He wrenched at the snap fastening. She was doing the same, grinning as she undressed, stepping out of her shorts and laughing.

And somehow they were in the water, their clothes a mess on the grass. "You said we couldn't afford to get them wet," she whispered, "So this is the obvious alternative, don't you think?" She sank to her neck in the water, pulling him with her.

"I think you're deliberately driving me crazy."

"Well, that, too."

They kissed again, with the fresh, peaty smell of the water

rising all around them. Lord, her body! He ran his hands over her, the water like cool satin, her skin taut and slippery. She wrapped her legs around him and the water supported them both. He could have entered her right here and now, but the pull between his urgency and this slow, cool, delicious fore-play was too good to lose. She held him—and he held her—in a state of sizzling, tingling expectancy and throbbing promise. Soon, soon, but not yet.

The sun angled lower and inched behind the tip of a pine tree. Breeze or no breeze, the bugs wouldn't stay out of the way for much longer. He saw some hovering inches above the water, drawn to their body heat. Shoot, they'd get eaten alive and he couldn't manage to care. *Eaten alive.* He must have said it out loud…

"Wait a little," she said, "we'll take care of it," and he didn't understand. What was she doing, wading those long, tanned legs out of the water, moving away from him when they were both totally naked and when his male intent stood out in the water like a submerged branch in a beaver dam? "Where are those matches we brought?"

"In the front pocket of my pack. Lannie?"

She just smiled, the lake water streaming from her body. "Wait. Come out and sit on the rock. Let the sun dry off your back. There's no rush. I'm lighting mosquito candles, that's all."

He did as she'd suggested, stood with the sun and breeze getting him dry and watched her helplessly, loving her naked-ness and her absorption in what she was doing. The sun etched her skin with fire. Her breasts made blue shadows that shifted every time she moved. Her bare feet were silent and almost reverent on the grass. The setting sun turned the colors of the landscape to vibrant green and pink and gold, while the fading breeze made goose bumps on his cooled skin.

She looked like some ancient goddess of nature preparing

a ritual, a rite of midsummer. She gathered up the half-burned citronella candles from inside the lean-to and brought them out to where he waited. There were eight of them. She set them in a circle, balancing them on rocks placed flat on the grass, then lit them with careful concentration, cupping her hand against the breeze that was dying away now, with the lowering sun.

"How is this?" she asked.

"It's beautiful." He couldn't keep his voice from cracking.

"Try it." She invited him into the circle of flickering lights and he smelled the citronella in the air. "Did I make our circle big enough?"

"Plenty."

He reached out to kiss her and hold her again, but she shook her head, maddening and fabulous in the same moment. "One more thing…"

"Wh—?"

"Two more." Lannie knew she was teasing him, and didn't care. She reached into the pocket of her shorts and brought out the foil packet and a tube of bug cream.

The foil packet was some strange foreign brand she'd picked up six months ago—no, ten—to cater for a wild fling that had never happened. To cut a long story short, the Australian guy she'd briefly volunteered with had seemed cute at first but then she'd seen him from another angle, and although she was by no means a virgin, she didn't hand out those kinds of favors when her heart and passion weren't fully involved.

End result, unopened packets of protection in her makeup bag that she laughed about every time she saw them, and she'd lost count of the times she'd almost thrown them away. Today, she'd wickedly put a couple—yes, more than one!—in her shorts pocket.

Lannie, Lannie, Lannie… Did you even dream the setting and the moment would be this good?

The bug cream had the same lemony scent as the candles. It was a herbal kind, without the chemical factory smell. She pooled some in her palms and rubbed it through their hair, hers first, then Nate's, then anointed his body with it as if it was a hallowed perfume, frankincense or myrrh, touching it to the pulse points on his wrists, the back of his neck, behind his knees, down his arms, across his shoulders.

"Not everywhere," she told him softly. "Because I want to taste you, too, not just the lemon."

"And chocolate," Nate murmured, completely helpless, not at all sure how he was going to hold onto himself another minute. "When you tasted of chocolate, just now, I nearly died of how good it was. Don't make me wait anymore, now, Lannie, because I don't think I can."

"No?"

"I can't. I really can't. You're killing me."

"Oh, Nate…"

She dropped the bug cream, wrapped her arms around him and didn't say another word.

He pulled her down to the grass, dragging hungrily on her arms, burying his face between her breasts as she fell against him. A second later he had the grass tickling his back and her breasts grazing his chest. She laughed about landing on top and he rolled her onto her back to assert a little mastery, pinning her with his elbows and swooping in to kiss her before she could protest.

Ah, she hadn't intended a protest. She wanted it as much as he did, reaching for his face and cupping it between her hands, pulling him closer, shuddering with need as he slid his body over hers, finding the place where his erection could nestle against her inner thigh. She arched against him as if their contact still wasn't close enough, and he had just enough control left to decide, no, not yet, not this fast, give a little more, first. Get that protection in place, and then give…

"Nate…" she urged him on a whisper.

He sheathed himself then slid lower and kissed her breasts with slow, tantalising heat, sucking their peaks until she writhed and arched again. Now, lower, lower. She grabbed his head with splayed fingers and gasped, her hips bucking and rocking in a dance of intense sensation. Oh, yes, yes, he knew she would react this way.

He stroked her with his tongue until she could take no more and pushed him aside, gasping his name, pulling him up so that his head pillowed between her breasts once more. The lemon scent of the air exploded around him more strongly than ever, mingled with the intimate scent of her body.

Inside her, he almost lost control in seconds, had to slow himself down, and those heroically deliberate thrusts threw her over the edge again. She grabbed his hips and fought him, pulling on him, demanding him to be faster and harder for her and he couldn't do that *and* keep himself from the brink at the same time, so he surrendered to the power and huge-ness of it and just let himself go, crying out, not consciously noticing the brief, light, tearing and twisting sensation against his swollen flesh, wanting her so much even as he had her, losing everything but the sensation and the release.

Chapter Ten

Lying in Nate's arms afterward, Lannie watched the light fading from the sky while he dozed.

She loved this.

Some women didn't, she knew. They wanted their man present in the moment, active, *talking,* even, but Lannie loved that there was no need or opportunity for words because Nate had fallen asleep.

It meant she had him all to herself.

She had *this* all to herself. The peace. The light ebbing in such beauty. The heavy warmth of a strong, beautiful male body to hold.

Nate's body.

It felt important.

Precious.

Unique.

Hers.

For how long?

Well, for as long as it lasted.

She felt a stirring of concern at this thought. He wasn't that kind of man, she was almost sure. He wouldn't have done this if it was going to be the one and only time. He was too cautious and forward-thinking for that. They'd explored this whole side of him, this whole difference between how he was and how she was in that area, and the stirring inside her was complicated and two-edged.

What a rare, fabulous thing to find a man who was that strong at heart, who had such a powerful, steady compass in his attitudes and feelings and beliefs.

Wow. Just wow.

She'd met so many men who were the opposite, who just didn't care or think or take responsibility for their actions or their emotions. Men who never grew up. Men who always blamed someone else for whatever went wrong. Men who thought it was clever to get a woman into bed with lies or trivialities or outright deception. Men who didn't want anything *but* to get a woman into bed, and cared nothing for what she thought and felt and who she really was.

Don't let this one go, Lannie.

So what was scaring her, right now?

Because, yes, she *was* scared. She recognized the fact that part of this stirring, part of the emotion unfolding inside her was fear, and she didn't understand it.

Nate took a big, slow breath in his sleep, a sigh of solid air. She slid her arm farther across his body, needing to feel more of that strong, solid, intensely reassuring weight. Oh, he was beautiful! So male and real.

The light had almost gone and the shadows made him seem heavier and even more powerful in his physique. There was a soft dappling of hair across his chest, and arrowing low on his belly. He had muscles that seemed as if they were sculpted from warm stone. He had flaws, too. There was a scar on his left temple, and his nose wasn't completely straight. She learned the flaws by heart and they became part of the things about him that were important.

Keep him, keep him, hang on to him, he's precious.

The candles flickered softly, doing their job, marking the circle of lemony, bug-free air. Lannie had made a magic place for the two of them with this circle and she wanted to stay in it until she'd worked this out. Worked out the fear.

It's me.

I'm afraid I can't match up. I'm afraid of how much he'll want. That he'll want me to be as strong and sure as he is, and I'm just not that person. I haven't needed to be. I've always had Dad to rescue me, or a first-class flight to get on. I've never had to live with consequences I didn't want. I'm afraid he'll see this in me, and try to be even stronger in compensation. I think he might be *too* strong, sometimes. He might kill himself with it. He might push himself and push himself, always the strong one, until in the end he breaks and it's my fault because I couldn't take my share of the load.

He was beginning to wake up.

Not yet, Nate, not yet. Stay sleeping a little longer for me.

She let go of the fear and seized on the last precious moments of silence and peace, of having him to herself without even him knowing. She laid her head on his chest and listened to his heartbeat, curved her hand around his hip bone and felt the webbing of muscle that surrounded it.

"Mmm…" he murmured a minute or two later, his voice a little creaky and as lazy as hell. "Hello, beautiful."

"Hi." She wanted to kiss him, didn't quite dare in case it betrayed too much. But he reached out and traced the line of her lips with his fingertips, inviting her mouth toward his and she couldn't resist. Just one kiss. A whisper of a kiss to seal the moment.

Mmm… But then his muscles coiled and he snapped back into focus.

"Wow, the light is almost gone." He sat up too quickly, as if he'd done the wrong thing in letting so much time pass. "I never meant to do that!"

"You're cute when you're asleep," she said, so he'd know he hadn't done anything wrong at all.

"We should—"

"I have the flashlight. It's not cold." A moment later, she heard him swearing under his breath. "What's up?"

"It broke. Shoot, it broke, and I didn't realize and just fell asleep."

"The condom?"

"Yes. It's torn."

"I'm sorry. Oh, shoot, I'm sorry! It wasn't an American brand. In fact, I don't know what kind of a brand it was."

"I think I felt it, right when— It didn't click, then, but—" He swore again, fierce yet inaudible. Lannie didn't need to actually hear the words to know what they were. She understood why he'd turned away from her, but it felt as if he was shutting her out, all the same. It broke the lingering mood of peaceful, precious happiness she'd wanted so much to keep and hold.

"It's okay," she said quickly. "It's fine."

"It can't be, can it?" His naked back said more than his voice. His shoulders had tensed and hunched. He bent and began to retrieve his shorts and briefs, as if covering himself as quickly as possible would somehow undo the other potential damage.

"It should be. It really should." She felt a ridiculous need to give him reassurance, and cursed her own happy-go-lucky attitude. The weird brand…she'd never been able to read the Use By date…and what was she doing, anyhow, picking up suspect condoms in Thailand for a man she'd never slept with and hadn't thought about in months, and then keeping them as if they were a quirky souvenir?

She'd picked the right time to come home. She'd done the right thing, wanting to ground her life a little more. She knew it. Now she just had to work out the details.

"I don't think we need to worry," she told him insistently. "I mean, unless you have something nasty you don't want me to catch."

"I'd be horrified if I did."

"And I've had a heap of medical checkups with all my travel, so I know there's nothing like that you're going to pick up from me. Please let's not—"

"No. I don't want to, either. Spoil it. No!" She could still read the tension in his back, the struggle in him. "It was too good for that."

"It was. It was." Thank you for saying it, Nate, but why are you still turning your back?

He circled around and came to her at last, torso still bare. He'd picked up her strewn clothes and footwear, which already felt cool to the touch. Nighttime dew had begun to fall. It would be chilly soon. "Here, we'd better get going."

She shivered suddenly in response. Yes, definitely chilling down fast.

"But, Lannie, you're telling me the timing is safe?" he said. "That's what has me concerned about this." He stood back, as if he might get her pregnant even now, just from looking at her the wrong way, or touching her hand.

She disentangled shorts from bra and T-shirt from hiking boots. "Yes. Don't worry. I'm sure you don't need the details on dates and cycles, but please..."

Please, please.

Put your arms around me. Forget this. I love that you're so responsible, but if it spoils all the good stuff, what's the point?

She hadn't had her period since flying back from Turkey, so it should come any day. Travel often stretched out her cycle by a couple of weeks. She seriously wasn't concerned. And she seriously wanted him to kiss her, but if he wasn't going to, then it was time to get dressed.

Finally, *finally*, when she had boots back on and underclothes, T-shirt and shorts, he came to her, buried his face in her hair and whispered, "I didn't trust myself to do this when it was skin to skin. Would have wanted to get you down in that grass with those candles all over again."

"I'm so glad you're doing it now. Nate, I'm so sorry..." She held him tighter, let his weight hold her up against gravity and make sense of her whole life. He smelled like childhood summers and sailing on the lake and picnics in the woods.

"Why? There's no reason for sorry. Sorry we did this? Sorry you're not ripping off your clothes all over again? No..."

"No, I mean the stupid condom."

"Don't."

"Yes. It feels like it was my fault. As if I was showing off. My exotic, interesting life."

"I never thought it was showing off. My ego was hugely stoked that you'd brought them, that you'd foreseen this and wanted it."

"I never foresaw how good it would be. I want it even more, now..."

"Don't make me kiss you here, or we'll never get back down that trail."

"Okay, I won't make you kiss me," she whispered, and they simply stood there, wrapped in each other's arms, with the citronella candles still flickering and the breath of dew falling on their shoulders. If the world had ended right then and there, Lannie wouldn't have cared.

Chapter Eleven

August, San Diego

"It must have been that very first time," Lannie said. "By the lake, with the candles. When the condom broke." That beautiful, beautiful day with its one jarring moment…

"But you had your period after that." Nate paced the room. "You told me you had."

After the way they'd silently held each other a few minutes ago, Lannie had hoped for greater closeness. Forgiveness. Shared understanding. But the distance had come between them again. They were reacting differently, thanks to their different histories—the differences so much clearer to her now than they'd been even three days ago—and she didn't know how to bridge the yawning chasm.

"It was very light," she told him. "I didn't think anything about it at the time. I thought it was the travel. But maybe it wasn't a period at all. I've heard that some women bleed after they've conceived."

"We have to get you a test." He was already striding toward the door, as if the possible pregnancy was a ticking bomb about to go off.

"Is that the most important thing right now?"

"Yes! We need to know what we're dealing with. It's pointless doing anything until we have the facts. The *fact*."

"Let me come with you."

"There's no need. There's a drugstore right around the corner. I'll only be a couple of minutes. You need to eat, settle your stomach. I'll be back before you know it and we can get this done."

Yes, great, but she didn't want him to leave at all. She didn't want his concern for her, or his need for certainty, to separate them even for a few minutes. Not until they'd talked more, and touched more. She hated these proofs of difference between them, in the way they thought and felt about things.

Alone, she sipped the tea and nibbled the crackers, and felt a little better. She let her head and heart explore the idea of adopting the baby out. There were so many couples who were desperate for a baby. She could bring a dazzling ray of sunshine to someone's life, while starting with a clean slate of her own. She could do anything. Go anywhere. She didn't have to submit to this radical change in her life if she didn't want to. She wasn't in the habit of submitting to things she didn't want, as Nate was.

She experienced a moment of dizzying relief at the thought of her potential freedom, but then, without warning, it changed to horrible vertigo. The room felt as if it was spinning around her and she panicked completely. Let her baby go to strangers? Carry it for nine months and then leave it like a piece of baggage in an Amtrak locker?

She didn't even know this child yet—couldn't be totally

certain that there even was a child—and yet the thought of giving it up, giving up a tiny, baldy boy who looked like Nate, or a red, wrinkled girl who might one day want to learn to dance or ride horses, was so terrifying and appalling and impossible that she had to cradle herself on the bed and hug the mattress so that the room came right again and her stomach stopped churning.

She knew she could never have done it, never have given a baby away. Even when she'd been thinking about it, it had all been a game. Let's pretend nothing in my life has changed. Let's pretend I don't have to do this…

No. Let's not. Let's not pretend.

What if I'm not pregnant at all?

But she knew that even the possibility of such a thing had changed things between herself and Nate forever.

He came back with a drugstore bag. "You okay?"

"Still a bit woozy." She lay sprawled on her stomach like a starfish, and he must have noticed the handfuls of sheet crumpled in her hands.

"Well, I have it, when you're ready."

"Why is the uncertainty killing you so much, Nate?"

"Because I like to know what I'm dealing with."

"Whereas I like to test out all the possibilities."

"What possibilities have you tested out so far?" He sat on the side of the bed, touched his hand to her back, but didn't leave it there. She was torn between craving the contact and needing their emotional distance from each other out in the open, unsoftened by the deceptive closeness of a caress.

"One, that we could adopt it out, but—"

The breath hissed between his teeth before she could keep going.

She told him, sarcastic and gentle, "Don't worry, that one didn't get very far."

"I would never let my own—"

"Can we stop with the righteous anger? Neither would I. But some people do, if they know in their hearts that it's the best thing for their child, and I think it's incredibly brave. Don't condemn the people who make that choice by condemning me for even thinking about it."

"Okay. Point taken. You're right. I tend to think everyone's a flake, sometimes." He touched her back again, and once more took his hand away too soon. "I should know by now that you're not."

"Thank you." She breathed again for a little while, feeling him watching and waiting and frowning, holding in his impatience.

"What else?" he prompted.

"That maybe I'm not pregnant at all."

"In which case, we're back to square one."

"No, Nate," she said. "We'll never be at square one again."

She remembered the things they'd said to each other weeks ago about first steps—the magic of them, the importance, the wonder. What step were they up to, now? You couldn't ever go back. Nate was right about that. She'd spent her whole adult life managing to stay a step ahead of unhappy consequences, while he labored under the weight of a whole raft of them.

Something had to change.

In both of them.

"You mean, even if you're not pregnant," he said slowly, "nothing is going to take away what we've said to each other about it, and how we've both felt?"

"That's right." She heard his hand crunching the paper drugstore bag, as if he might toss it in the trash. "But still, we need to do this, don't we?" she conceded, understanding a little more about his need for answers. "Find out for sure?"

"I think so."

"Okay, hand it over." She slid off the bed and stood up, took the bag, went back into that damned bathroom and closed the door behind her.

Chapter Twelve

July, Upstate New York

When a phone call from his mother began with singing, it was never a good sign.

Today the song was "Chapel of Love," bouncing jauntily into his left ear as he sat at his desk at ten at night going through some numbers he should already have been fully on top of—blame beautiful Lannie for the fact that he wasn't!—and he experienced a sinking sensation of dread low in his stomach as soon as he recognized the melody and the words, and considered their significance.

Gonna get married.

Please, Mom, no, not that…

He remembered what he'd said to Lannie several weeks ago. *Weddings bring out the best and the worst.*

"Guess what, honey?" Mom trilled. Was it technologically

possible for a woman of fiftysomething to flutter her eyelashes through a phone line?

Nate heard himself come out with all the right clichés. He was very happy for her. He couldn't wait to meet Cole. He was sure the man would make her very happy. It was wonderful news. He hoped they'd be very happy together.

Those words *very happy* somehow kept cycling through his responses despite his best efforts to come up with something original and he wasn't surprised when his mother said reproachfully, "I thought you'd share my joy, Nate. Why can't you ever celebrate the things I do? This is one of the happiest days of my life."

The best and the worst.

She applied this kind of emotional blackmail all the time. If he wasn't ecstatic about her choices, it was his fault. If he pointed out some crucial detail she hadn't considered, he was just a thorn in her side. She preferred him to fake his way through the right phrases rather than express what he really thought. The old *raining on her parade*.

"I am happy. Of course I'm happy. Very happy." What kind of a mother *wanted* her son to lie to her? "But you haven't known him all that long, and—"

"Four months."

Significantly longer than he'd known Lannie, he had to admit. His ego told him this was irrelevant. He wasn't in the habit of screwing up his life the way Mom did. He made better choices. Still, he tried to soften his tone. "And I haven't met him, so it's a little hard for me to—"

"But you will, at the wedding."

"Yeah, but that's a little late for me to scope him out and discover he's a con man or a sleaze," he answered, not soft at all, then realized that he'd neatly trapped himself—or had Mom done the trapping for him?—into attending the happy event. He added quickly, "Not that I'm necessarily going to be able to fly—"

Too late.

"So you're coming, then? You are? You've made the decision already? You normally like to think these kinds of things over for about a hundred years."

"Yeah, because—"

"Oh, that is wonderful! I didn't want to ask, or let you see how much I was counting on it. Put pressure on you, you know. Cost you expensive flights and hotels." Which had to be the first time in her life that Mom had expressed qualms about costing him money.

"When is it?" he asked, through gritted teeth. "Do you have a date set?"

"The third week in August. The 21st."

"That soon?" It was only just over six weeks away.

"We don't want to wait."

No, Mom, you never do. Heaven forbid you hold back long enough to spot the cracks in your fool's paradise. No, just rush right in, and then feel this helpless, naïve, fatalistic astonishment when it crumbles around you a few weeks or months later, and never, ever learn from what just might have been your own mistake in the first place. And your intentions are always good, and you're a good person, and I can't just stand aside and let the disaster unfold.

He called on his experience of all the wedding-obsessed brides who'd passed through the Sheridan Lakes hotel over the years, in a last-ditch attempt to mount a convincing counter-argument, at least wait long enough for the stars to fall from her eyes. "But Mom, does six weeks give you enough time to organize the dress? The photographer? The cake? The reception menu? Will you find a decent venue that's not fully booked up, at such short notice? How about choosing a ring?

And a cake? And bridesmaids outfits? There's a lot to do for a wedding."

"Oh, we're going to make it simple. We're having the ceremony and the reception in the bar. All I care about is that you'll be there, Natey-pie. And at our age, there's absolutely no reason to wait, and every reason to start our joy as soon as we can."

"Of course. Yes." He sighed through his gritted teeth. "You said the 21st? That's a Saturday?"

"We're thinking six o'clock for the ceremony, followed by cocktail hour and photos, then dinner."

"I'll try to come out a few days ahead." In time to have a couple of meaningful exchanges with Cole—he didn't even know the man's last name—and hopefully find out in time if there was anything truly sinister in his background.

A light knock sounded at the office door. He covered the phone and went, "Yup!" and there was Lannie, ready to report on the lavish Sweet Sixteen party currently spilling out from the hotel's pool area and onto the lit-up southern lawn.

"Should I come back later?" she mouthed.

He shook his head, indicating she should wait. Three days since their hike, and his groin still surged every time he thought about what had happened beside the mountain lake, with the scent of citronella and chocolate on their skin.

They'd lingered over dinner that night, only leaving the restaurant because they were the last couple in the place and they knew the staff would be wanting to close up. On the way back, they'd passed the turn off to Musk Lake, and he'd told her, "I have a piece of land down that road, where I want to build a log home some day. It's not on the lake itself, but it has the most incredible views."

"So you really plan to stay here permanently?" she'd asked. "Sheridan Lakes isn't just a stepping stone for you, toward managing a big city hotel? You don't want to get to New York?"

"I don't want to live in the city. Even if I don't stay with Sheridan, I'll stay in these mountains. Have my own place, maybe. Twenty rooms and a three-star restaurant. The kind of place movie stars come for fishing or boating, but don't use their real name in the guest register."

"I want to see your land."

"The house isn't built yet. Neither of them are built. Not the log home, or the boutique hotel. It'll be a while, even for the house."

"Still, I want to see where it will be."

But it was dark and late—it wasn't possible that night. He'd brought her back early the next morning before breakfast— they both needed to be visible and busy at the hotel by eight— and they'd walked all over the four-acre plot while he showed her where he planned to build.

He wanted a great room with a stone fireplace and a loft area for an office or study. He wanted a timber deck and floor-to-ceiling windows facing southwest to the view. Beside the deck, he wanted an infinity-edge pool, filled by water running over natural rock. Below all of this, there'd be a tangle of garden that shaded off into the woods, so you couldn't tell where his plantings stopped and nature took over.

His pants got drenched in dew from the long, wet grass, and she took off her shoes and went barefoot. She took pictures of him gesturing at the view, and of the morning sun slanting through the grass, of the dark backdrop of pines and the rocky outcrop near the top of the property where garnets gleamed in the dew-wet, weathered stones. He took pictures of her standing on the rocks, and one of her with three garnets in her palm. He'd pried them loose for her.

"Gemstones," she'd said. "You'll be rich."

"They're not gem quality, too small and crumbly. You saw

how easily they came free, all powdery at the edges. But I like them, especially if the rocks are wet and the sun is shining at the right angle. It's like my land is decked in jewels."

And right as he said it, the sun had crept onto the rocks, showing the translucent red crystals, and she'd clasped her hands together. "Wow! So beautiful! I love that they're hidden. The moss and lichen half covering them. I wouldn't have seen them if you hadn't shown me."

"Don't tell anyone," he'd said, like a kid after showing his secret treasures, almost anxious about it.

Don't spoil it.

Don't tell.

"No," she'd agreed at once. "Nobody would understand."

Which told her that she *did.*

They'd arrived back at the hotel twenty minutes late, stomachs empty, racing to catch up all morning, and he hadn't cared. It had been such a perfect start to the day. And now here she was, waiting for him, with the same glow around her that he still felt in his heart from that morning.

"That would be fabulous, sweetheart," his mother was saying. "Oh, I'll be so thrilled if I get to spend some time with you, and Krystal will be over the moon, too."

"Uh, yeah, and what's his last name, can you tell me?"

Silence.

Shoot! He knew at once that he'd been too obvious. Lannie's entrance had distracted him. How could his mother be this savvy about his verbal subtexts and so clueless about everything else in her life?

"You're not going to do it, Nate," she said, deliberate ice in her voice. "You are *not* going to have him *investigated,* and then throw it in my face that he's been in prison for unpaid parking fines, or, or..."

"Has he been in prison? For anything?" He watched Lannie trying not to listen, trying to work out who he could possibly be talking to, if a subject like prison had come up. And who he could be talking *about?*

"No! He has not been in prison!" Mom said.

"Do you *know* that, or—?"

"Of course I know it!"

"Because he's told you?"

"Why would he tell me? Do you go around telling people that you *haven't* been in prison, that you *don't* have terminal cancer, and *don't* owe a hundred thousand dollars in unpaid child support, or *don't* have— Sheesh, Natey! He's told me about himself, his whole history, and I trust him with my heart, with my life, and if he hasn't mentioned any of those things you're hoping to find—"

"Not hoping to."

"—by siccing some shady P.I. onto him, then it's because those things don't exist. Okay?"

"Okay," he conceded.

"I hope you're ashamed of yourself."

"Ashamed of caring about your well-being? Well, no, I'm not."

"Ashamed of having so little trust. In anyone. I am not telling you his last name and giving you that kind of ammunition!"

"I wish you'd have a little less trust in people you've known for four months and a little more trust in your own son."

There, Lannie, this is my mom I'm talking to. We had the best time of our lives, three days ago. Now, welcome to the other part of my world...

Down the line, his mother sighed, and dropped her voice to a whisper of emotion. "I know you care about me, Nate. You're good. You're better than I deserve. But so is Cole. And I can't wait for you to find that out for yourself."

"I'll be there," he promised. "We'll talk detail in a few days, when I've looked at my schedule and checked out flights.

Meantime, all my congratulations, and let me know right away if anything changes."

"You mean if we call it off?" she drawled.

Yes, actually, but you wouldn't want me to be honest enough to admit it.

"I mean if you can't make the bar work for that date and have to push it back, or something."

"We're not changing the date. We'll get married on the beach, if it comes to that."

"I have to go, Mom. Talk soon, okay?"

She told him she loved him and was proud of him and they ended the call. And she *did* love him, and she *was* proud of him, but her behavior and her thinking killed him all the time, brought his bank balance back to zero on a regular basis, gave him a hundred sleepless nights a year, and it was the same with his sister Krystal, and they were his family and he had a duty to them and there was nothing he could do about it.

"Whew!" he said to Lannie. "Sorry. She—my mom—had some family news. It's never a relaxing conversation."

"No?"

"I'll tell you, sometime." I won't hit you with it yet. I don't want you running a mile. "How's the party?"

"No problems. They're having a ball. I wanted to make sure you weren't still in here working."

"And here I am, still in here working."

"You're catching up after Wednesday. I'm a bad influence on your work ethic."

"You're terrible. Next you're probably going to want me to come grab a beer in the bar with you and I just won't be able to say no."

"You want a beer in the bar?"

"I would kill for one. I'm almost done here, and the rest can wait till morning."

"Mmm, I really am a bad influence."

"Yeah, don't stop, please."

She laughed, and the moment caught and held and they just had to stay that way, grinning at each other with wide, moony, happy smiles, and the only reason he wanted it to end was because he wasn't close enough to her right now to touch. Or kiss.

"C'mon," he said impatiently, pushing himself up from the desk. She came toward him and slid her arms around him, and he knew he wasn't leaving his office just yet.

In the bar, fifteen pretty fabulous minutes later, she said to him, "Tell me about your family. What was your mom's big news, and why were congratulations in order, with prison mentioned in almost the same breath?"

Okay, so maybe he'd have to hit her with some of it tonight, after all.

He took a pull on his beer as he thought about how to say it and what to say first, and decided on the simple version. "She's getting married…"

"Oh, lovely!" She clapped her hands together and threw him that smile.

"…*a-gain.*"

"Oh."

Weddings. The best and the worst.

"And I haven't met the guy, and her judgment isn't always what it should be…" Another pull on the beer. He told himself to slow down. Maybe Cole was a really great guy.

Lannie watched him, reading his face like a book. Her eyes looked dark and serious in the dim corner of the bar. "So you want her to be happy, and you hope he's never been in prison, and she doesn't appreciate that the subject of prison even came up."

"Yup. Good summary."

"And you told her you'd come to the wedding."

"If I can. That's up to the hotel calendar, obviously."

"And when you get there, you'll try to convince her to call it off if the guy doesn't come up to scratch."

"Only if it's serious."

"Define serious." She sat forward, resting her chin on two sets of folded knuckles. "Are we really talking prison?"

"Depends on the *reason* for prison," he explained, and watched her eyes widen.

She wasn't from his world, and sometimes it showed.

He remembered what Mom herself had said, and clarified, "Like, if it were for unpaid parking fines I wouldn't make it into a big deal."

He hesitated for a moment, then bit the bullet. Lannie needed to know. Keeping his family out of the equation was no better than Mom wanting him to fake a celebration of all her bad decisions. If the Sheridan Hotel heiress was going to stay in his life for any length of time, she had to know what his life was really about.

He said deliberately, "Drug dealing or armed robbery, on the other hand, would be more of an issue. Her second ex-husband—my father was the first—is still behind bars for both of those. She's…kind of conveniently forgotten about him, even though he's my sister Krystal's father, and focused on ex number three, who would have been actually a decent guy apart from his incurable gambling addiction. He filed for bankruptcy three times while they were married. I don't even know where he is, now, and I don't think Mom does, either."

"Right." She stayed silent for a minute, absorbing this. Then she went flippant on him, as if she knew he didn't want to go into too much more detail. "Gee, maybe my Dad wouldn't have gotten on my case so hard if I'd had those kinds of reasons for breaking my engagement."

"You've been engaged?"

"Yes, since we're doing a few revelations tonight. It was a

long time ago so there's no lingering after-burn. Walton was a very suitable guy. So suitable I practically threw up every time I had a meeting with the wedding planner."

"So what happened?"

"I told everyone the wedding was off and left the country. England is gorgeous for picnics in May."

"Nice save."

"But Dad still gives me grief. About that and the MBA."

"Yeah, I heard about the MBA."

"Well, you know, it was *boring,* and I really only did it for Dad, and I'd learned everything I wanted to know, and I didn't need the actual piece of paper, and one of the professors looked like he was about to get a little too keen on helping me with my assignments. Plus—as I may have said—France is gorgeous for skiing in March."

Nate laughed.

Happy.

Light-headed.

Unexpected, really, when he'd been so tense after his mother's call.

The beer?

More like the relief of knowing he'd said some stuff that needed to be said about his family, and Lannie was still sitting there, looking beautiful, smiling at him, lips all soft and sweet, mocking herself a little, daring him to question her choices, and she hadn't hammered him for every little sordid, pathetic detail. He could hit her with a more thorough version later on, when she was already somewhat prepared, and he felt a surge of optimism that she would handle that, too.

She was a pretty strong person.

She was amazing.

"After the beer, do you want…?" he began.

And she squeezed his hand across the table, leaned closer and whispered, "Yes! Oh, yes! I want!"

Chapter Thirteen

August, San Diego.

"It's positive," Lannie announced.

"Are you...?"

She cut him off, sharper in tone than she'd meant to be. "Don't ask *am I sure,* okay? I'm sure. As you've recently said, not everyone in your life is a flake. Here it is. Read the instructions and take a look for yourself." She thrust the plastic wand toward him. "The line is so purple it's almost black. And even though the instructions don't say that blackish purple makes you more pregnant than pinkish purple, I think it's a fairly safe bet."

She sounded like a witch and hated herself...hated him a little, too, because this *wasn't* just about her. It really wasn't!

If they could have had a do-over on this, she would have taken it in a heartbeat.

Let's just go back to that moment when I looked at my blotchy face in the bathroom mirror and first put all those little clues together. Only this time I won't be scared and unsure. I won't think back to the massive breakdown in communications we had on Friday night, the real, meaningful differences in the way we think about things, and wonder how in the heck we could dare to bring a baby into the world, and could dare to think we might do a good job of it, when we haven't begun to sort ourselves out yet. I'll just pretend everything's fabulous and fully under control right to the point where it explodes in our faces, the way Nate's mom and sister do, and we'll go from there.

"Can we start again?" Nate said, his voice low and serious, and the words so exactly the ones she'd wanted to say herself that she burst into tears, the emotion like an ambush, unsuspected one moment, all over her the next.

"Yes, please!"

"Ah, hell… Ah, hell…" He threw the test in the trash, took her into his arms and crooned in her ear. Curse words, but they sounded like words of love because he meant them so much, he was as helpless as she was, she knew it. He *wanted* all of this to be okay, just as she did, even when it wasn't.

She let herself go and sobbed, just sobbed, didn't even try to stop because crying felt…good.

Weirdly.

Hormones, or something.

No, it wasn't just hormones. It was the way he held her, so tenderly, so much care, kissing the top of her head, whispering to her that they'd talk, they'd find a way through, it didn't have to be full of conflict and uncertainty. She felt safe and precious in his arms as the minutes passed. She could smell his familiar scent, feel his breathing, hear his voice in his chest.

If she could just keep on crying forever, then they could stay like this, they wouldn't have to start on the hard part—working out the rest of their lives.

She couldn't keep crying forever.

The sobs evaporated as suddenly as they'd started. She gulped the last one back, and her breathing steadied, even though her face must be a nightmare.

He had tissues.

He must have reached for them at some point while she was crying and she hadn't even realized. He held out a huge, thick, aloe-softened wad of them, from the elegant dispenser on the wall beside the king-size bed.

"Here, sweetheart…"

She buried her face in them and he dabbed at her eyes and nose, kissed her trembling mouth until she responded with sweet, desperate heat.

"Take your time," he whispered.

"Thank you." For the tissues, for his patience, for his arms around her, for his lips on hers.

"Then I have something important to say." This time the words dragged out of him, spoken too slow and too heavy. "The only thing that's possible."

Something important.

The only thing.

He was going to ask her to marry him.

She knew it, suddenly, with the same absolute certainty given ten minutes ago by that dark, dark purple line.

He'd held her in his arms while she cried. And while she'd been wallowing in hormones, he'd been thinking through the options, and, being the man he was, he'd stoically, stubbornly decided to do the right thing—as he'd said, the *only* thing that could possibly make her parents happy about a grandchild, the thing that would sort everything out on paper, while ignoring all the stuff that a piece of paper could never solve.

She didn't want him to do it.

Not with such a leaden, negative motivation.

She didn't want to even hear the words, to watch him saying something he *never* would have said at this point, after so little time and space to think, if the test hadn't come up positive, saying it out of duty and responsibility and honor and obligation. He lived half his life that way. His family tortured him thanks to his sense of obligation, and now that she'd seen this firsthand in all its pitiful detail, Lannie wasn't going to—

"Lannie…" A controlled release of breath. "I think we should get married."

There.

Done.

Said.

His voice was heavy, serious, joyless.

There.

Done.

The way he'd probably written out the check for Krystal this morning, and handed it over.

"No. No. No!" She pressed her palms to her ears and shook her head, both actions too little and too late.

You see? You see what I mean? You see what he does to himself?

The words yelled themselves silently in her head, as if to God, or to her best friend Jane, as if someone had been in the room listening to all this, a secret audience, and she'd warned them in advance what would happen.

She couldn't stay in the room another second. Pulling away from Nate, she half fell around the corners of the big bed and headed for the door. There was a pair of her shoes sticking out of the partially open closet door. She bent down, scooped them up by the thin straps, reached the door, wrenched it open and just ran. Barefoot. Toes curling in the thick, luxurious carpet of the hotel corridor.

Of course he came after her. "Lannie! Atlanta…! Please!"

"I *cannot* deal with this now!" she yelled back at him. "I need space. I need the ocean. I'm going to go walk, and, and, *breathe*. Think about what a terrible thing it would be, Nate, to do it for a reason like this."

"For our baby?"

She stopped, softened a little. "There's this thing they say to you in aircraft safety announcements, Nate, you must have heard it, for if there's an emergency and the oxygen masks drop down. *First put on your own mask, then assist your child.* We're not doing it for our baby if we're not, first of all, doing it for ourselves. Think about the iron bands you put around yourself. I don't want to be another of your iron bands. I will not be. I won't join with your mother and sister in bringing you to emotional ruin, like the three witches in *Macbeth*."

"So you're just going to *run?* That's your answer? What, the San Diego waterfront is gorgeous for walking in August?" Oh, yes, she remembered saying those lines to him about her past escapes to London and France.

She stopped, faced him, her voice thick with tears. "I have to do this. After what happened Friday night, and yesterday, everything I saw, everything I understood about your life… I have to do it. And you need it, too. I have to give this to both of us. The space. The time."

She turned away from him, not knowing, this time, if he would follow her. At the elevator, she slipped her feet into the shoes, then went down to the waterfront and walked in them until she had blisters on both heels.

Chapter Fourteen

August, Upstate New York

"Come to my mother's wedding with me, Lannie."

Behind him, a jazz singer crooned a sultry ballad and forks chinked against cake plates. He and Lannie had been sitting quietly together—not to say hiding out—for several minutes, talking a little but not too much, and it had suddenly seemed like the right time for biting down on a bullet he'd been thinking about for a while.

"I thought you'd never ask…" Lannie answered, with a tease in her voice.

"I'm serious." *If you knew the doubts I have about this…*

"So am I. It's only two weeks away. I started to think you had another date already lined up for it."

He pushed the doubts to the back of his mind and took on her light tone. "Yeah, about six hopefuls waiting for my call in California, but I couldn't pick between them, so you're the lucky one who gets the gig."

"I love it when you get romantic on me, Nate."

"Well, you know, all the ceremonies and receptions and engagement parties we have around here, it hits you both ways. Sometimes, I don't want to have to look at another bridal chair cover or six-tier cake as long as I live."

"We're not looking at them. We have our backs to them. We're looking at the lake." It was softly clothed in darkness, in the deepest, most velvety, layered shades of midnight blue, scattered with lights here and there, on the water, the islands, the shore and in the overhead, like Van Gogh's famous painting of a starry night.

"Sometimes, though, beyond all this detail and decoration, it kind of…it actually…"

"Sometimes it's actually romantic and beautiful," Lannie said softly.

Weddings. The best and the worst.

They'd both had no problems managing today's big event. The couple had been cooperative and appreciative, the catering had run smoothly, there'd been no embarrassing relatives to cause a scene…

Which brought Nate back to what he'd just asked Lannie. "I take it you're saying yes to the California trip?"

"Of course I'm saying yes. I'd love to come to your mother's wedding with you. Heck, I'd love to come on a community-service trash-collecting mission with you."

"What a lovely thing to say, my dear…" he drawled, Rhett Butler style.

"Hey, it really is a lovely thing to say, because I mean it, and I know you're not asking me on a whim." There was a tiny pause. "I know you're a little scared about it, too."

How is it that she *gets* that, he wondered? Am I that obvious about it?

She reached out and found his hand, threaded her fingers through his. They were seated side by side in two of the slope-backed wooden Adirondack chairs that the hotel grounds staff kept in scattered, inviting groupings on terraces and decks and promenades all around the resort.

"I know your family has some problems, Nate," she said. "You've let enough of it slip. Kind of doled it out in measured doses like medicine, but I haven't spat the medicine out yet, have I?"

"You haven't actually met them yet." He was astonished that she'd picked up on the doling-it-out thing, also. Once again…he'd been that obvious about it?

"You seriously think I might run for the hills when I do?" she asked him.

"I think family is important. I think they can make or break—"

"Not when it's this good." She squeezed her fingers tighter in his, and he squeezed back. "They can't break it when it's this good."

They can't break it when it's this good.

Yessss! His heart pumped its fist in the air. Nate, you crazy fool, hearts don't have fists. But it was how he felt.

A winner.

Dizzy with the victory. Illogical with it. Wild.

Just happy.

This good. This good.

But even so, her confidence killed him sometimes. It killed him now, as soon as the sense of victory ebbed a little. It was such an in-your-face reminder of how different their lives had been. They had a ton of things in common now, for sure. The *now* of their relationship had his head spinning with happiness every minute of every day, and he was pretty sure she felt the same.

But they'd come from such radically different places.

She'd had her needs met since before she was born, he
goals supported, her whims indulged. She'd been taught t
believe in herself, and life had proved that she was right to d
so. She'd been taught that even when things didn't work ou
the way you wanted, there were alternatives, and they wer
usually better.

He, on the other hand, had been his family's most reliabl
breadwinner for more years than he could count. He was th
one his mom had sent to the drugstore, at the age of twelve
to buy a pregnancy testing kit. He'd had to "lend" her th
money for the purchase, out of the earnings from his pape
route. Result: his sister Krystal. For the testing kit, he wa
still owed.

And he'd lost count of the times he'd had to run interfer
ence with the debt collection agencies looking to collect o
his mother's unpaid bills. Those guys weren't such bullie
over the phone to a kid whose voice hadn't broken yet.

He'd told Lannie some of this, and other stuff.

Not the pregnancy test story.

She'd listened. She'd said all the right things.

But talk was cheap.

Who should know better about this than Nate himself, sinc
he'd been listening to his mother's cheap talk about her plan
and her problem-solving for as long as he could remember?

This was why Lannie had to come to the wedding. She ha
to live this part of his life, not just hear about it at second
hand, thinking it was all in the past.

He cleared his throat. "I'll make reservations for us."

"You haven't made one for yourself, yet?"

"I wanted to wait until I'd asked you, to make sure we coul
get the same flights."

"Will we stay with your mom, or…?"

See, she didn't get it.

She had no idea what it would be like to stay with his mon

The cramped clutter. The mess of papers and knick-knacks and packing boxes everywhere. Even though Mom hadn't ever stayed in any one apartment for more than a couple of years, she'd managed to accumulate a scary amount of junk and it came with her, move after move after move. Decaying show costumes, sentimental souvenirs, broken household goods she vaguely thought might one day get fixed, toys that Krystal had outgrown ten years ago.

Sometimes he tried to get her to go through it all, only keep what was important, maybe make a little money with a garage sale. But in her starry, sentimental eyes, it was *all* important. He would spend five hours sorting through it with her, and she would come up with three paltry items that she could bear to let go. She would never accept that so much sentiment was a luxury she couldn't afford.

"No, I'll find us a hotel. A good one." Sheridan Hotels hadn't gone into the San Diego market yet, but he knew of a couple of great places in the downtown area or out at Coronado Beach.

Would Lannie push the issue of staying with his mother? He waited, but she didn't say anything, just twisted those fingers through his in another caress.

He loved her.

He knew it.

He hadn't said it to her yet, but he wanted to.

She was so *right*. Listen to that silence! She knew when not to talk. She knew there must be some issue about staying with his mother and she had the sense…the sensitivity and generosity and care…not to prod and push for the details he couldn't bring himself to give.

"There's something else we should do…" she began after a moment.

"Yeah?"

"Go out somewhere with my parents, when they're here. It's

going to be a proper visit this time. They're actually coming to see their daughter, it's not just Dad flying in and out for a meeting. I'd like the four of us to spend some time together see how we all get along, even if we present it at first as business rather than personal."

The family thing cut both ways. She was right about that

"They're coming Thursday?"

"Through Monday."

"Sunday night, then? We have functions every other night."

"Sunday for dinner. How about that place we went the first time, along the lake? Paradise Point. That was beautiful."

"Call them and make sure they keep the night free. But yeah, maybe don't mention in advance that you and I are seeing each other."

"Let it come up naturally, over the meal?"

"Low-key. Pick our moment. By the end of the evening, I'd want them to know."

"I thought you might want to roll through a plate-glass window to escape the whole idea," she suggested, half teasing half not.

"A plate-glass window, to escape dinner with your parents? To escape telling them that you and I are involved? Dramatic escape bids aren't my style."

"No, they're not, are they? You won't admit that you're nervous? I am!"

"Might admit it. Won't act on it."

"Are you nervous?"

"Yup."

She only laughed.

Lannie might have laughed when the dinner-with-parents was still eight days away, but by the time they actually got to

Sunday evening, she was more nervous than she'd been since… sheesh…since telling Walton that their wedding was off.

No. She hadn't been nervous that day, because she'd been so sure she was doing the right thing. In which case the last time she'd been this nervous was the day of their engagement party. She resisted the idea that this might be significant in any way.

Her parents had been at Sheridan Lakes for three days by this time. She'd shopped with her mother, had a mother-and-daughter salon and spa date, and played eighteen holes of golf with both her parents. Mom boasted a mean handicap, but Dad had chased her down to come in three strokes ahead. Lannie brought up the rear on the scorecard by a wide margin, but on the plus side had only lost six balls to the water or the shrubbery.

"Those are coming out of your allowance, young lady," her mother had teased her. "I told you you'd never make that chip shot on the fourteenth, thankless child."

Lannie liked her mother.

Loved her, too, of course.

But *liked* her, which she had a suspicion was a rarer thing. Love in families was something you could get stuck with even when you didn't want it. It could hold you in chains. Liking was different. Liking was a choice, a good thing.

But it said something about judgment and trust and respect, too. When you liked someone, it was partly because you trusted and respected them, you valued their judgment.

Lannie trusted and valued her mother's judgment and… okay, getting to the heart of it now…this meant that Mom's opinion of Nate Ridgeway was *important*.

It really mattered.

Her stomach lurched. She'd been thinking about this all day, on the golf course this morning, in her office as she looked at the draft text for the hiking tour brochures, and in the shower twenty minutes ago. Now, standing in front of the mirror while she put the final touches to her makeup and hair it hit her why she was so nervous about tonight.

If Mom doesn't like him, it'll really matter to me. It'll change things. It might change everything. Because I'll start to wonder what she sees about him that I don't, and I'll wonder if it's something I should *see, and what will happen when I do...*

A knock sounded at the door.

It would be Nate himself, she knew, come to collect her. Her parents had gone down to Saratoga for a late lunch with friends after the round of golf, and were meeting them at the lakefront restaurant. He was early, she realized, and wondered what that said about his state of mind.

It took her a moment to answer. She actually looked across at the French doors leading out to the deck and considered an escape. Not a permanent one. Just a chance to sit out there for ten minutes and settle her spirits. He would come back, or she could reach him on his cell. He was the one who'd arrived before the agreed time, after all.

But in the end she called out, "I'm here, Nate!" and went to let him in.

And the second she saw him her heart melted and her legs went weak.

I'm in love with this guy...

He looked so good. He'd brought flowers, not a big, showy bunch that might have graced the concierge desk in the hotel lobby but a whimsical, woodsy arrangement far better suited to her summery lodge.

"Oh, I don't think there's a vase..."

"There is now. On loan from hotel housekeeping." He produced it from behind his back and stuck the flowers into it with no water and she laughed at him.

"This is your idea of flower arranging?"

"This is my idea of time management."

"You're early…"

"Not early enough, if we have to footle around arranging thirsty flowers." He bumped down the vase onto her little dining table and pulled her into his arms with a rough, cheeky confidence that caught her in so many ways—caught her attention, her curiosity, her heart.

He'd said a week ago that he was a little scared about tonight, the way she was, but there was none of that in him right now. Instead, he sizzled with energy and heat. He believed in himself, he wanted her, and he didn't mind letting her know about both.

"What's happened to you, Nate?" She couldn't help laughing, felt him sweeping away all the negative emotions inside her, the nerves and jitters and doubts, and it was wonderful. His energy was like a force surging into her. His confidence was as tangible as the muscles of his back beneath her hands.

She thought, why have I been so scared about this? Mom is going to love him to pieces. Dad already thinks he's worth his weight in gold.

"*You* happened to me. I was focusing on tonight, rehearsing how I was going to prove to your parents that I'm, you know, not an axe murderer or a weasel in human form, and then I thought back on these weeks we've had. I thought about you. How you look in shorts. How you smile. The way you think. The way you make feasibility studies sexier than a push-up bra, even if it was you wearing it."

"Wearing the feasibility study?"

"Wearing the bra. I'm making a mess of this."

"Keep going, and I'll tell you at the end if you're making a mess of it."

"And I just thought, it's going to be okay. We're good together. That's the heart of it. We're good together, and they'll have to see it, and if they don't then it's their problem not mine. That's the end. How'd I do?"

"You didn't make a mess of it. You made me believe it." She kissed him, a warm, appreciative smack on the mouth.

He caught her jaw between his hands. He wasn't in the mood to accept smacking kisses. His was slow and deep, a seduction as sweet as thick honey. "Did you not believe it before, then?"

"I was a little jittery."

"I can help with that…" His hands slid down her back and he marked her neck with a sizzling trail made with the touch of his mouth. The jitters evaporated and turned into something much stronger and better.

Still, she wanted him to understand. "My mom's never met you, you see. It's important."

"This is important." Kisses on the slopes of her breasts. Kisses on her mouth.

"You're right." Oh, she couldn't fight him anymore. Not even to get her point across. Did she have a point? Or was it the same as his? "This is us, and we're great," she finished, believing it as much as he did.

"Good," he said firmly, "Because we're running out of time… Definitely no time to take it slow."

"No?"

"No."

"Fast is good. I love f—" She didn't even have time to say the full word.

It was swallowed by a gasp as he found the zipper at the side of her dress and slid it down, peeled the floaty dress fabric up, up, tickling her stomach, whispering past her thinly covered breasts, over her head, onto the chair.

Didn't bother to remove her underwear.

Was too busy removing his.

Fast.

Following the dark pants and buttoned shirt already flung carelessly on top of the discarded dress.

"Now…" He took her breasts in his softly cupped hands, his thumbs like pads of velvet over nipples that had peaked to hard beads through the chocolate satin fabric of her bra. "Now…" He brushed his groin across her stomach and she felt his impatience and readiness, matching her own.

Fast could be good.

Fast could be very, very good.

Why hadn't they tried fast before this? Just because they'd been too busy trying everything else…

She gasped again as he brushed aside the triangle of fabric that covered her mound. The satiny, lacy thing was tiny, stretchy, chocolate like the bra, and no barrier at all. He'd come prepared. No suspiciously unreadable brand name and Use By date, this time. She'd thrown those out the day of their hike and hadn't looked back. They'd made love in her bed late at night, in his bed in the middle of the afternoon, beside the hotel pool at two in the morning in the dark, with the security cameras turned off and a tiny sliver of moonlight finding its way onto the heated water. But this…

"Now?"

"Yes, yes. Oh, I'm so ready… I'm *so ready*…" She was shocked at herself, deliciously, wickedly shocked. She wanted him so much, the urgency itself was a huge turn-on, building the storm wave of need almost to breaking point in mere seconds.

He was so strong, hoisting her onto his hips, holding her backside in his cupped hands while she wrapped her legs around him, thrusting into her as soon as she'd opened for him, finding her slick readiness without a moment's pause.

Oh, fast was *gooood*.

She clung to him, met his thrusts with a hungry, grinding, softly swollen pressure that made him groan and hiss. "Now? Right now? Oh, it's too good. Oh, Lannie, if you don't make me slow down this second—"

"Don't slow down. Please…don't…slow…down."

He couldn't have, even if she'd asked for it. But she was a thousand miles from asking. She was a thousand miles from anywhere, and so was he, in a universe of their own where nothing mattered but this. This. This.

She wanted to cry out but muffled the violence of the sounds against his shoulder, opening her mouth, almost biting him. He kissed her neck, strained with his arms to hold her as they spent themselves, then he collapsed his chest against hers, against that dark, satiny bra twisted but still in place.

When he slid out of her and set her gently on her feet, she couldn't let him go. She was shaking and so was he.

Shaking and laughing, both of them.

Exultant, happy, embarrassed in a good, giggly way.

Pretty damned pleased with themselves, actually.

"That was…athletic." She heaved out a breath.

"It was amazing. You were amazing."

"You were. So strong. To hold me like that."

"Hell, I never wanted to let you go. I'm still not letting you go."

"No, me neither." She pressed her head against his chest, felt him kissing her hair and lifted her face so he could find her mouth instead.

He ran his hands down her back, found the tiny stretch of fabric still pulled out of place and hooked his fingers into each piece of lace and elastic to put them where they belonged.

"And to think I'd only just changed," she whispered.

"Mmm, are we late yet?"

"Not yet."

"Good." He kissed her a little more, just held her, until

finally they knew they had to move and dress and go to meet her parents.

Lannie had her happiness written in every line of her body, and she didn't care if it showed to the whole world.

Chapter Fifteen

August, San Diego

"Honey, I just wanted to come by and say thank-you for lending Krystal that money. It'll make a real difference, a huge difference."

"It's only four thousand dollars, Mom." She set Nate's teeth on edge when she was like this. It was one of her regular roles, and one she felt sincerely—devoted, sacrificial parent, brushing aside her own needs and disappointments and pain to focus on the happiness of her family.

"Are you sure you can afford it? I mean, you've already given me—"

"Look, it's okay. It's fine."

"And—and—I hate to ask, but you know I'm going to have to. The suppliers—"

"I know. I'll take care of it."

It set him back—again—in the fulfillment of a long-held

dream, but he could deal with that. The log cabin in the Adirondack woods that he would build from his own design could wait a little longer.

He knew Krystal would never pay him back, and neither would Mom. They'd have the best of intentions at first. Maybe they'd even send a hundred or two. But then things would spiral out of control again, and both of them would stop thinking about repaying the last loan and start thinking about when they could ask for the next one.

And always, *always,* they were sure that the next one would be the turning point, the fresh start, and soon, in their fantasies, they'd have millions in the bank and would shower Nate with cash and gifts and a lifetime of repayment, and all the damage they'd inflicted—on themselves more than on anyone else, but he couldn't seem to convince Lannie of that, she persisted in thinking *he* was the one who'd suffered most—would be magically undone.

"It'll change everything, give her the fresh start she needs," his mother gushed.

She looked tired, as if she hadn't slept, and there was something courageous about her, despite everything. If she'd been cruel or calculating or incapable of love, he might have shaken off her dependency with a cold shoulder and no regret, he might have stopped trying to compensate for her poor judgment and rash decision-making, but she wasn't a bad person and he loved her, and that made it so much harder.

"Thank you so much," she continued. "She has worked so hard. It's not her fault that things haven't panned out the way they should have. If anything, it's mine."

"Don't make a big deal out of it, Mom. Don't blame yourself." He didn't want to talk about any of it, right now. Lannie had left an hour ago and she still wasn't back. She hadn't taken her cell phone with her and he was starting to wonder what he'd do if she just didn't show up. For all he knew, she could have rented a car and embarked on a cross-country road trip.

If she did show up…*when* she showed up…he didn't want Mom here, he wanted him and Lannie alone, so they could deal with the fact that he'd asked her to marry him and she'd put her hands over her ears and told him, "No!"

"Where is Lannie, anyhow?" Had Mom read his mind?

He exerted massive self-control and kept his voice and body language casual. "She's gone for a walk. She wanted some air. I might go find her in a minute. She'll be somewhere along the waterfront."

"What time's your flight?"

"Not until late afternoon, getting into Albany tomorrow morning. We have a late checkout, and it's only a short cab-ride to the airport. We really don't need to leave here for another hour." He'd been reminding himself of this for the past forty minutes.

"I'll get out of your way, then. I need to go open up the bar for the cleaners. You'll stop by to say goodbye on your way to the airport?"

"Didn't I say we would?"

"Are things okay between the two of you, baby boy?"

"Yes, of course."

"I've been concerned. I know you can't have hoped these past few days would pan out the way they did. You've both been looking tense and stressed. Especially Friday night. I saw you walking down the street together, not touching each other…"

"We had some stuff to work through. We still do," he admitted, the words breaking out of him half against his will.

"Oh, Nate…"

"Right now, I'm not sure if we can." Hell, he *really* hadn't meant to say that! Shoot, *why* had he said it?

He waited for the storm of advice and platitudes and

gushing support to break over his head, but it didn't come. Instead, his mother engulfed him in one of her hugs, big and too tight and over-scented but warm and full of love. "You can," she said simply. "You will. I know it."

Chapter Sixteen

August, Upstate New York

Lannie's happiness with Nate did show.

Far too clearly.

Her mother picked up on it within their first five minutes in the restaurant, and what worried Lannie the most was that Mom didn't say a thing about it, and she couldn't understand why. It would have been so easy. A quick trip to the ladies' room together, or a few steps away from the table to look at the view of the lake.

They'd had all sorts of heart-to-hearts together while shopping, on the golf course and in the salon. They'd covered Mom's concerns about Dad's health, and the options for retirement they were considering. Mom confessed that the thought of taking one of those permanent staterooms on a luxury cruise ship gave her the horrors and she thought Dad would hate it even more, but he had the misguided idea that it would allay her fears about his health and she didn't know how to talk him out of it.

They'd spoken about Mom's health, too. Lannie had convinced her to get a skin blemish on her arm checked out and use sunscreen more often on the golf course, the daughter-knows-best stuff that Mom actually liked, she'd confessed. "It makes me feel cared for and loved, having my own child giving me lectures about taking care of myself."

And Lannie had even hinted that she was dating someone and it was going well, and Mom had tried to get her to say more, so shouldn't she have at the very least now shot her a private smile behind their restaurant menus, or given a cryptic tease, just *acknowledged* the whole thing in some way?

Instead, her eyes had gone wide, she'd frowned and pressed her lips together, then—even worse—hidden her reaction behind that conveniently huge laminated menu and only emerged from it a couple of minutes later to make a random and unnecessarily soothing remark to Dad about golf, before disappearing again.

She has doubts.

Serious enough doubts that she didn't want her daughter to know about them.

Mom hadn't suspected for a second that Lannie meant Nate, with those earlier hints. As Lannie and Nate had planned, Mom had thought they were making a foursome tonight purely for business reasons. She'd placed Nate in the "senior Sheridan employee" pigeonhole, and she was shocked to discover so quickly that he might actually belong in the "someone my daughter cares about" pigeonhole, where there was already Jane—whom Mom loved—and just a select few others.

The waitress came to take their order, which robbed Mom of the protection of the menu, and took away any lingering sense of safety in Lannie, too. Nate didn't realize that Mom had guessed, and Dad hadn't seen a thing. Her father was struggling with his dinner choice, a little irritable about it, which told Lannie he wasn't feeling one hundred percent.

She patted her stomach and sent a questioning look to her mother.

"His heartburn," Mom mouthed. "Don't talk about it."

Lannie nodded, her jitters only increasing. Mom had guessed and was shocked, Dad was viewing the whole world through heartburn-colored spectacles, Nate was fielding Dad's barrage of questions about hotel business with efficient good humor, but Lannie knew, because they'd talked about it, that he didn't want to make this dinner too much about work.

It wasn't a harmonious grouping.

"And for my entrée I'll have the seafood linguine," Dad announced to the waitress.

Mom stifled her protest, but got her point across anyhow, purely with her body language. A rich wine and cream sauce, when his stomach was already playing up? Was that really the wisest idea?

Dad glared at her. "I took another pill."

"Those pills aren't a free ticket to eat whatever you want."

"Well, they should be!"

Then Mom came right out and said the *S* word.

Salad.

"That's what I'm having," Lannie chipped in, as bright as a Christmas tree ornament. "The chicken Caesar." She meant it as a distraction, but Dad heard it as her siding with Mom against him.

Before he could come out with another irritable line, Lannie whipped out the draft hiking brochures from her purse and dropped them on the table. One of them fell in her water glass, and since it was a draft and had been printed on basic copy paper on her office copier, the colors immediately began to run.

She fished it out. "See what we've been working on?"

"I don't know why you're wasting your time with this, Lannie," her father said, "When you could be doing so much more. We have Sheridan Chicago opening next year. You could manage that, if you had the right experience in place from running Sheridan Lakes. It would have been the perfect stepping stone, and you've just handed it back."

He thumbed at Nate, seated to his left, without looking at him, as if handing back Sheridan Lakes had been akin to throwing pearls to swine. The comment and the gesture were an insult to both Nate and Lannie, but she didn't mind on her own behalf. She knew Dad's moods, especially the heartburn-influenced ones.

But she minded for Nate.

"You have a massive inheritance riding on how you handle these next few years," Dad went on, before she could find a response. "Are you going to let everything I've built run itself into the ground within a few months of my going to my grave?"

Mom pressed her lips together. If he was that concerned about going to his grave anytime soon, he could order the darned salad!

"We need to talk about all of that," Lannie said, attempting to find the right place in between upbeat and soothing. "But I don't think now is the time or place. Let's enjoy our meal. And…and Nate's company."

Mom went onto a higher level of alert. Was that the pressure of her knee under the table? Lannie ignored her.

"He's come up with some great ideas for the wilderness packages. He wants to use a seasonal approach. Winter tours as well as summer ones. Spring and fall, too, because each season has something different to offer up here. The seasonal thing was his idea, but I'm working on the details now, and I think the brochures look great. If I was managing the whole hotel, there's no way we could put any of this in place by the end of the year, but this way, because it's my main focus, we can, and I think it'll have a significant impact on our occupancy rate during what have traditionally been our low seasons. Not that I want to just talk business tonight…"

She let herself look at Nate and the smile came onto her face all on its own. She hadn't put it there. It just wanted to be there, and it was.

Mom's knee mashed into hers once again, this time with bone-jarring force. *Your father is not in the right mood for this,* yelled the knee.

"I can't help that, Mom," she said behind her hand. "I refuse to tiptoe around it. When are we next going to be together, the four of us? When will there be another opportunity? Can't I talk about being happy?"

"Not if you want him to be," her mother muttered. "He has huge ambitions where you're concerned, honey, you know that, and I have to say I think he could be right. And tonight, when he's been feeling off color since golf, is just not the most tactful time."

"What's this about?" Dad said.

What it was *about,* Lannie suddenly saw, was her mother sitting right there, in front of Nate himself, and saying virtually straight out that someone who merely managed one of the family's hotels—and only a "stepping stone" hotel at that—wasn't good enough for the only daughter of the empire.

She hadn't done this right, she realized. They shouldn't have made it a dinner. Her parents ate out all the time. They were as jaded in spirit by lavish restaurant meals as was Dad's poor stomach. Instead, she and Nate should have taken them out into the mountains to show them some of the trailheads, the vistas you could see on those tiny back roads. They should have finished with a simple picnic on Nate's stunning piece of land with its pines and green grass, the lake and mountain views, the garnets gleaming in the rocks.

Then they would have seen what Lannie herself saw—not just Nate's hard work and talent in running the hotel, but the man he was at heart, a man who needed wilderness and physical challenge the way some men needed beer and TV sport, a man who dealt patiently and honorably with family problems Lannie had only just begun to fathom, a man who'd built himself and his own life the same way he would one day build his beautiful log home—with his own hands and his own vision and his own heart.

They'd blown it, doing it this way, so formal, so lacking imagination.

She'd blown it, knowing Dad as well as she did, knowing how conservative he was about decision-making and plans, and knowing how unreasonable and tunnel-visioned he could be, especially when he wasn't feeling well. She should have thrown open a new window, letting her parents know about Nate, instead of treading the same old ground. Shoot, she still remembered every moment of the starched and uncomfortable engagement dinner she'd had with Walton and both sets of parents.

Nobody had answered her father's question, and the silence had begun to stretch out.

Nate took a breath. "Sir," he said, "Lannie and I wanted to tell you something tonight."

"Tell me what?" Without waiting for an answer, he appealed to Mom, chafing his stomach with the heel of his hand. "Linda, shouldn't our appetizers get here soon?"

"It's not that long since we ordered," Mom soothed him. "And they're busy in here tonight." The reassurance was delivered absentmindedly as she sat on the edge of her seat, waiting for Nate's announcement as if it was a grenade with the pin already pulled.

"We're dating," Nate blurted out, thrown by the sidebar about the appetizers.

"Yes," Lannie came in, as if this would help.

"Dating?"

You know, Dad, going out, doing fun things together, seeing each other even when we don't have to, finding out what's underneath...

"You mean you're getting engaged?" he asked.

"No, Dad, just dating. At this stage."

"Then why are you making it into an announcement?"

"Because we wanted you to know," Nate came in.

"Know *what?* Lannie, you know I hate this modern ambiguity, this inability to commit. You've had a broken engagement, you've had those others, Daniel and Gordon and whatsisname—"

"Bill..." Mom warned, but was ignored.

"Since you're obviously never going to take a blind bit of notice of my opinion on the kind of man you should be looking for, why put us through the torture of having to make friends with all your missteps and mistakes?"

The unfairness of it was like a slap in the face.

Make that four slaps.

One each for Walton, Daniel, Gordon and Blue.

Lannie was twenty-nine years old. Four boyfriends since the age of eighteen, including one fiancé, and now Nate. Not such a lengthy roll call of names, and yet Dad had managed to make it sound as if she bounced from man to man without ever knowing her own mind.

She stood up. "Mom, can you please give him about nine more tablets for his heartburn? I'm done here. We'll talk about this some other time. It wasn't a good idea, tonight." Then she pushed her chair out of the way, turned on her heel and threaded her way between the crowded tables toward the exit.

Sometimes, a point had to be made as forcefully as you possibly could.

Was he supposed to follow her? Nate wondered, watching her retreating figure with its squared shoulders and long legs and shapely, swaying butt in that filmy, pretty dress he'd pulled from her body so recently.

He felt angry and embarrassed and torn in two. He knew why she'd left. Her father had been pretty unkind, and beyond tactless. An only child was entitled to behave like a prima donna under such circumstances, possibly, but where did that leave him? Bill Sheridan was hardly likely to distinguish him from the collection of "missteps and mistakes" if he made an abrupt exit, also.

He was surely obligated to stand his ground.

Show that he was his own man.

Not a pushover.

Worth something.

"She…uh…has a habit of leaving this restaurant early, with insufficient warning," he said, because he had to say *something*, and flippancy seemed better than the other options.

"Oh, you've been here before?" Linda Sheridan inquired. It sounded like polite small talk, but there was a subtext.

"We've eaten at most of the decent places along the lake," he answered. "I like to keep tabs on the competition, for one thing. Paradise Point is one of the best, in my opinion."

"And for another thing?" Bill prompted.

"I'm really serious about your daughter," he said simply. "I spend as much time with her as I can."

"You're crowding her. Bulldozing her."

"I'm not. Because I think she's really serious about me."

"But you're not engaged."

"One step at a time."

"Now, see, this is what I—"

"Bill, for heaven's sake, he's not saying he can't commit!"

"Then what the heck *is* he saying?"

"Just what he said. They're taking things one step at a time. Of course they need to get to know each other. Would you want our daughter to rush into something like this?"

Nate didn't know if Linda was implying something, there—namely that if Lannie didn't rush, she might have time to realize he wasn't good enough for her.

"I like to know where I stand." Bill added irritably, "Nate, could you go fetch her back, please?"

It was a command, not a suggestion, he recognized, and hoped his reluctance didn't show as he stood up.

Would she even be there? She could have called a cab, or taken his car. He'd given her a set of keys.

There you go, Bill, exchanging car keys. Is that commitment?

"Back in a minute," he muttered aloud.

"Thank you for putting up with us," Linda Sheridan said, with a splash of wry humor in her voice, just enough to give Nate some faith that she wouldn't be the mother-in-law from hell, if they ever got that far.

The *if* loomed large, right now.

Outside, Lannie was halfway up the private road leading out of the resort, striding along beneath the overhead lights that marked the way and turned the dark asphalt to silver-gray. Her heels almost struck sparks from the ground. He had to run to catch up, didn't want to call out too soon because he didn't know if she'd be willing to wait. Maybe she really had called a cab, and it was picking her up on the main road.

"Lannie…" He was out of breath by the time he said her name. He'd sprinted the last hundred yards, and was amazed that she managed such an impressive pace in those strappy pumps.

She turned. "I thought you'd be right behind me." It was clearly an accusation.

He kept himself from biting back. "And when you found I wasn't?"

"I kept going."

"Was that really the way to handle it? How do you think I felt, stranded there?"

"You should have left with me. Presented a united front. Made a point. Mom and Dad had *no right—!*" She clenched her fists at her sides and growled like a bear, furious and frustrated, gorgeous and electric in her anger, her eyes even more vibrantly blue than usual. He could have kissed her…

Still, he held himself in check. "It was mainly your Dad, wasn't it? I don't think he's feeling that well."

"I know he's not. But that's no excuse. And it wasn't just Dad, it was Mom, too, only she didn't let it show. Why do they have these *expectations?* These narrow, tightly defined boxes they insist on putting me in, every single time there's a life choice at stake!" She ground the tips of her fingers into her temples.

"Because you're their only child. They have all their eggs in one basket. And they have a really big pile of eggs."

"You sound as if you're on their side." Okay, she'd begun to calm down a little. She was listening.

"I'm trying to see things from their point of view. I pretty much had to, left alone with them."

"What did you say?"

"That I was serious about you."

She lifted her chin. "And what did you get in answer to that?"

"Your Dad kind of warned me not to bulldoze you."

"Oh, great. See? I'm glad I didn't hear that."

"So you left me to hear it instead."

"Back to that, again."

"Yes, because it matters. It's important. It's not the first time you've done it."

"Oh, because I didn't want to let those intoxicated guys spoil my dessert, a few weeks ago? I told you, I pick my battles, and that one just wasn't important."

"I was thinking about the engagement, and quitting Harvard without the degree."

"You didn't know me back then. You don't know what was going through my head. What's the point of sticking something out when it's not working?"

"Pride, maybe? Proving something to yourself?"

"There was nothing I needed to prove. I like to make a clean break, and a quick break. I like to act on my realizations."

"What if your standards for what's working and what's not working are way too exacting and high? What if nothing can ever work as perfectly as you want it to, so you never see anything through? What about riding out the bad patches until they come good again? Or keeping working on something until you *make* it good?"

"Is that what you're saying we should have done tonight? Stuck it out until Dad took another handful of antacid tablets and turned into a human being again?"

"Yes. I think that's what I'm saying. But you left me to do it on my own."

"So why are you out here now?"

"Because he ordered me to go after you and bring you back."

"I'm not going back."

"You need to come back in there with me, Lannie, and finish this."

There was an intensity in Nate's voice that told Lannie he was serious. Her stomach lurched and went queasy. She felt so keyed up and on edge, unusually volatile in her emotions, daunted by the prospect of *riding it out* the way Nate believed they should. In the end, it was the queasiness that made her give in. She just didn't think she could argue this out any longer without getting physically shaky, or throwing up.

Nate seemed so strong and sure of himself, standing there. She didn't want them facing off like this. She wanted them to be a unit again.

A team.

Connected.

Touching each other.

She reached out for his arm, crisp and smooth and solid in its neat shirt. "Okay. We'll go back in. Can we have a minute first?"

He knew what she wanted. "'Course we can have a minute…" he whispered, and she melted into him, felt the queasiness subside, felt a flooding wash of well-being just at the way he felt and smelled, at the sound of his voice vibrating in his chest.

He touched her as if reclaiming her, running his hands over all his favorite places, pressing his mouth to her neck and then brushing her lips, tasting them, unfurling her kiss and deepening it until they both began to lose their breath.

"We're flying to California in four days," he said. "That's going to be important, too."

"And fun, I hope."

"Fun," he agreed. "It better be that. Until then, let's…" He trailed off, searching for the right words.

"Ride it out?" she suggested, giving him his own phrase.

"Yes. Ride it out. Make it work."

"Maybe those antacid tablets will have kicked in."

"Maybe your Mom will have made him change to salad or vegetable soup."

"Oh, yeah, in your dreams, buddy. That's right up there

with me dressing in a gorilla suit and beating you with banana leaves for your intimate pleasure."

"What, you don't do gorilla suits?"

"You *want* me to do a gorilla suit?"

"Depends. First, tell me what the gorilla would be wearing…"

"Is this how we ride it out?" Because, beyond tension and queasiness and gorilla suits, she really wanted to know. "By laughing about it?"

"It's one of the ways," he said. "A great way, actually. Pity it isn't always possible."

Chapter Seventeen

Nate and Lannie's flight left Albany, New York, at around ten on Thursday morning. They changed planes in Dulles, Washington and landed into San Diego at around three, Pacific time. Nate had made reservations at a stunningly revamped downtown hotel, where Lannie immediately felt both pampered and at home.

The day of travel had tired her more than she would have expected, and she put it down to the general tension she'd been feeling over the past few days. Her parents had left on Monday morning, both of them also flying out of Albany airport. Dad had been chauffeured to Albany by a hotel staffer at the crack of dawn. He had a week of business meetings in Europe, with a view to expanding the Sheridan hotel chain into Britain, France and Italy.

Mom wasn't going with him, but was returning to their home base in Upper Saddle River, New Jersey, just one of the three residences they kept. She would be meeting Dad out in the house in Aspen, Colorado, on the weekend. Lannie drove her to Albany, heard her itinerary for the next couple of months and privately thought it sounded way too complicated and unnecessary, all the shuttling between Jersey, Colorado and Florida, not to mention side trips to Sheridan hotels in other locations when Dad especially requested his wife's company. If the family corporation expanded into Europe, as well…

Lannie and Mom had talked during the one-hour drive, of course, and this was where the tension came in. She couldn't remember back on the conversation word for word, but certain moments stood out.

"Your father thinks you can do better, that's all," Mom had said at one point.

"Better for who…m?" Lannie headed off the possibility of a grammar lecture just in time, by remembering to add the final letter.

Not that Mom was pedantic about such things, she just believed a person's speech should match their upbringing, their ability and their education.

Which meant the use of words like "whom" even when no one else used them.

And apparently a person's choice of life partner should match their upbringing, ability and education in exactly the same way.

"Better for yourself, in the long term, obviously, honey."

"But what if *better* isn't what I want? What if the kind of better you're talking about is actually boring and soulless and stressful and pointless?"

"Are we talking about poor Walton again?"

"You should be glad I can learn from my mistakes."

"Dad didn't mean—"

"Missteps and mistakes. He said it. And Dad *likes* Nate."

"As senior management potential, not as a future son-in-law."

"You are backing us both into the corner of an engagement and marriage when we are nowhere near that far along. Nate would never ask me to marry him without feeling that we're both on really solid ground. He's just not like that. You would love how risk-averse and responsible he is, how much he thinks things through."

"So this'll be another bail out, sweetheart, if it doesn't work?"

"Better to do that, even if it's for the tenth or twelfth or twentieth time—which in this case it's *not*—than make a mistake that'll haunt me my whole life."

"You mean you're already seeing an end to it?" Was that hope and relief she'd heard in Mom's voice?

"No!"

She couldn't remember where the conversation had gone next.

Still about Nate.

Still about her choices.

In hindsight, she could think of six or seven issues or assumptions she should have called Mom on, or probed into more deeply. Why didn't Dad think Nate could work as a future son-in-law, when he worked so well in management? Just what sort of a man would be "better" in his eyes, when she'd already proved that she wasn't the kind of woman who went for the buttoned-up, trust-fund-endowed, screamingly suitable type, like *poor Walton* had been?

Poor Walton was currently worth around eight hundred million dollars, according to various rich lists, and the very thought of having to manage all that money and make it keep growing and growing and pointlessly growing forevermore… bored her to death!

Life could be simpler than that.

Life *should* be simpler than that.

Or Lannie wanted hers to be, anyhow. She understood this suddenly, in a way she never had before. Simple. Beautiful. Harmonious. Work that she enjoyed but that didn't kill her with stress. A home that didn't have to be a palace. A mountain log home, for example, built to a unique design.

Okay, yes, that's right, that was where the conversation had gone next.

She'd tried to explain this to Mom—the simpler life thing, downtime and fresh air and laughter—but Mom had argued that lack of ambition was a character flaw, at which Lannie had said, okay, well, she, Lannie, was the one who had the flawed character, in that case, because she was the one who lacked ambition.

Nate had plenty of it.

He'd worked his way up from nothing.

And then Mom had said something like, so, did that mean Lannie's idea of the perfect man was one for whom a hand-crafted log home in the woods was—you can't be serious—*aspirational?*

Well, yes, actually.

"And it's not exactly going to be two rooms with a dirt floor."

After that, they just got snippy with each other. How many bathrooms did a log home need in order to qualify as sufficiently upscale for the Sheridan hotel heiress? How many weeks in a year, Mom, was the Aspen place actually used?

Finally, Mom had admitted, with her hands pressed against her face. "You know what, Lannie? I don't really believe half of what I'm saying, here. I'm channelling your father. I'm really worried about him, honey. He just doesn't know how to slow down. I don't want this Europe expansion, but it's as if he's on a treadmill—a gold-plated treadmill, I guess—and you're right, *why?* And I buy into it for a while—ambition *is* a character strength—and then I think, no, there has to be something else. Maybe someday soon when we have…other priorities…to think about…"

She didn't say the *G* word.

Grandchildren.

But Lannie knew it was on her mind.

Talk about mixed signals and a whole new raft of things to stress over!

"You look tired," Nate said to her, as she pivoted aimlessly in the San Diego hotel room, looking at the view from the window without really seeing it, taking in the seductive softness of the huge pillows and wanting to bury her whole body in them right now, noting the pristine marble in the bathroom and wondering if this place had a good housekeeping team. He gestured at their bags standing in front of the mirror-fronted closets. "Do you want to rest while I unpack?"

"Are we seeing your mom and sister tonight?"

"I have to call them and arrange something. It's always too hard to plan ahead. I'm sure we will."

"Okay, then, yes, let me rest for a bit, then I'll take a shower to freshen up. I don't want to yawn through the whole evening and have your mother and sister thinking I'm bored."

She kicked off her shoes, lay on top of the thick white cotton quilt and closed her eyes, thinking she would relax rather than sleep. Oh, but this was so good…so restful…so perfect…

So nice to feel herself letting go of all the questions raised by her parents' visit. They seemed to float away with the low, cool-breathed hum of the air-conditioning.

She did sleep.

Heavy and long.

She didn't realize how heavy and long until she felt Nate's

warm body cradling her from behind. "I hate to have to do this…" he said softly.

"Wh—?" She rolled over to face him, her face feeling creased and stiff and her limbs sluggish.

"I arranged to meet Krystal and Mom and Cole at their bar at seven. I thought you'd be awake long before that, but it's six now and I know you wanted to shower and change first."

"It's six, already?" Her voice creaked, and even now her eyes didn't want to open. When they did, she saw that the light in the room had changed, becoming mellower and less direct because the sun had moved farther around the hotel building.

"You've been asleep for almost two hours."

"Sheesh, I had no idea I was so tired. I haven't slept well since Mom and Dad left. Even when I've been with you," she added softly. "I guess it's that. I'm catching up."

"Should I have woken you sooner? You looked so peaceful."

"Have you been creeping around trying to keep quiet?"

"No, I went down to the lobby and had coffee, made the dinner arrangement with Mom, went for a walk along the waterfront. It's warm, but the breeze was great. Maybe we'll grab some time for sightseeing while we're here, if things don't get too crazy."

"How likely are they to get crazy?"

But he didn't reply to this. Before he could, there was a knock and a call of, "Room service!" and he went at once to open the door. He'd ordered a snack of turkey club sandwiches and fresh-squeezed juice, and Lannie realized how hungry she was—way too hungry to wait for a late dinner—when she saw the food and the tall glasses of juice.

"Do you want to eat before or after your shower, Lan?"

"Right now, I think." In her head, the question about his family's craziness still hovered, but she didn't want to ask it again. She'd been half-joking before. Now, if she repeated it, she would sound as if she seriously feared that things might get ugly or weird.

They ate together, talking about what they could see in San Diego in just under three days. Balboa Park, Old Town, Coronado Island, Mission Beach.

"We do have a rehearsal dinner and a wedding to go to," she reminded him.

"Tonight, too," he said, sounding a little tight about it.

"You're looking forward to seeing them?"

"Yeah, I always do, and then I always…" He didn't finish, and once again she decided not to push.

They arrived at the bar promptly at six. It was in the revitalized Gaslamp Quarter, which meant a lot of tourist traffic, but also a lot of competition, and Lannie could see right away that Belle and Cole's place wasn't going to bring enough people in.

The building must be over a hundred years old, full of beautiful period detail, and the bar could have been given a warm, traditional atmosphere, but instead Cole and Belle had chosen to go contemporary with their recent revamp and the amateurish decor didn't work. There was a bar directly across the street that had the same hip, contemporary feel, but it was sleek and lavish in how it had been done, and anyone who wanted hip would go there, not here.

Still, there were a couple of groupings of drinkers, and Nate's mother was tireless in her bright attitude. Lannie liked her. She'd been inwardly very, very scared that she wouldn't, and that it would show, but you couldn't help liking Belle. It was the same as you'd feel for a stray puppy with a ton of personality and no house training. She warmed your heart and then…disaster.

Krystal, too, around twenty-two, sweet and naive in a lot of ways, with big, bouncy ambitions, and an incongruous hard-edged streak that showed in some of her conversation and spoke of life lived a little too rough and a little too close to the brink.

Cole showed up late, full of apologies, beer on his breath. He must have been incredibly good-looking as a young man but he looked seedy now—dyed hair thinning, clothing size in denial about the budding paunch. He had Paul Newman blue eyes, and he knew it, using them shamelessly to gaze into Belle's face as he apologized for his tardy appearance.

"Meetings, sweetheart, you know how they run late. I got caught up. Tried to call. Your cell was switched off."

"Was it?" Belle said, and rummaged for it in her bag. "No, it was on. Well, it's on now, anyhow. I called the florist, I guess I must have switched it back on then. I'm sorry, honey."

Cole pumped Nate's hand, said too many of the right things, leered at Lannie in a sneaky way that no one else saw, turned to Krystal and pawed at her a little. "Things are really gonna start happening for you soon, baby. That's the meeting I was in."

"You mean my portfolio, and my style consultant?"

"We'll make appointments for next week."

"Because I gave you the money three weeks ago."

"Next week, okay? These things take time and finesse to set up."

Krystal turned to Lannie and Nate. "Cole is having me do a whole new portfolio. Seven or eight different looks, to show my range." Her conversation went this way for the rest of the evening. "Cole says it's vital for me to…" and "Cole wants me to…" until Lannie wanted to grab her by the shoulders and tell her, "Enough about what Cole wants. Are you thinking any of this through for yourself?"

Belle beamed at everyone, managed the food which was appearing too slowly from the kitchen out back, and chipped in a few "Cole says…" speeches of her own.

"This time in two days I'll be Belle Mickinder," she said at one point, with a happy sigh, and the bar food was good enough to enjoy, and the noise level rose to a pleasant pitch. "We're going to make a profit tonight!" she concluded.

But Nate was quiet on the way back to the hotel. They'd walked, rather than taking a cab.

"Pretty good, wasn't it?" Lannie ventured to ask. "I liked your sister, and your mom."

"I found out his last name," Nate answered, off the point. He was walking too fast for her, striding as if in a hurry. She had to take a skip step every now and then, to keep pace.

"Did you find out how to spell it?" she asked him. "It's unusual."

"It was on the liquor license on the wall. I wrote it down." His face was set hard, words escaping from between clenched teeth.

"You're really going to do some research on him? Before the wedding?"

"I have to. The bar is bleeding money. If tonight counted as a good night..." He shook his head. "And didn't you hear what Krystal said? That she gave Cole the money for the photo shoot and the style consultant three weeks ago, and nothing's happened yet? Hell, Lannie, I'm so sorry. I'm so sorry to bring you anywhere near this stuff."

"I liked them," she said again. "I *liked* them." She linked her arm through his and tipped her head onto his shoulder, but they were walking too fast for her to keep it there.

"Yeah, but they're bad news."

They made love back at the hotel.

How could you not, in such a gorgeous bed?

But it was almost too intense. Lannie wanted to communicate with every touch and kiss and whispered word how much she felt for him, but he was locked away somewhere. Even when he shuddered into her and cried out her name and lay with his face tucked into the curve of her neck like a sleeping child, he seemed locked away.

Later, unable to sleep, she felt him climb out of the bed and disappear into the bathroom, where a light beneath the door and the clicking of his laptop keyboard told her he was researching "Cole Mickinder" on the Internet in the hope of finding out enough shady detail to put the brakes on his mother's wedding.

Chapter Eighteen

"He'll be here soon," Mom said, reassuring herself more than Nate.

Cole was already embarrassingly late.

The wedding party and close family had been scheduled to meet at the bar at six for the wedding rehearsal, followed by the rehearsal dinner at seven. It was now ten after seven and the guests who'd been invited for dinner only had taken their seats at the tables. There was a sign on the main door reading *Closed For Private Function,* which meant yet another night when the bar would run at a loss. Tomorrow night would be the same.

In some ways it made sense to have the ceremony and reception here, avoiding the expense of someone else's function center and getting their meals at wholesale rates, but Nate did the math and realized that a simple dinner for family at a local restaurant would have allowed this place to stay open for paying customers tonight instead of Mom feeding a whole bar full of dodgy friends and relations—Cole's "business associates," three of Mom's cousins who only ever seemed to show up when they could drink on someone else's dime, a handful of struggling actresses and singers that Mom had fallen in and out with over the years. There were around sixteen people here, in addition to himself and Lannie, Krystal and Mom.

Lannie looked fabulous tonight, as always, in a shimmery pinky-gold dress, her hair twisted into a knot high on her head, her smile in place every time it needed to be.

They'd had a great day today, waking very early with their bodies still on East Coast time, exploring the gardens and museums of Balboa Park, and lunching at one of its best restaurants. Nate hadn't wanted to spoil the mood by talking about the hour he'd spent in the bathroom last night, exposing all of Cole's secrets via the magic of the Internet. When he'd crept back to bed, she'd been breathing with a deep, steady rhythm—fast asleep, thank heaven. He didn't need to tell her.

He hadn't said anything to Mom yet, either. He didn't even know if there was any point. It wasn't as if she'd taken notice of such damning facts about her man of the moment, in the past.

"Maybe we should circulate the appetizers and drinks," Nate suggested to her. "We can't keep everyone bored and hungry."

"Five more minutes," Mom said stubbornly, and turned to Reverend Beale, from the church she sporadically attended, to make her third or fourth apology to him. He was officiating tomorrow, and clearly would have preferred a chance to talk quietly to the couple about the sacrament of marriage rather than standing around pretending to party in the absence of the groom.

Ten minutes later, Cole still hadn't shown, and Mom conceded that they had to offer food and drink. "We'll have the actual rehearsal between courses. It won't matter."

Between courses, still no Cole.

No Cale or Kyle, either. Would Mom want to know that he went by three different names? Did she know already? And what about the documented complaints from clients regarding his numerous past businesses, in and out of the entertainment and hospitality industries? What about the unpaid debts?

"You've tried calling him, obviously."

"I think there must be something going on with his phone."

He took a breath, ready to bite the bullet. "Mom, I did a little research last night…"

But Lannie, who had slipped unobtrusively back into the kitchen, returned to report, "Chef says the chicken is starting to dry out."

"Thanks for that." He squeezed her hand, hating that he was subjecting her to this. It was so familiar to him but she'd never dealt with it before, and the minute-by-minute reality was so painful sometimes.

"It's fine." She beamed at him, but the smile didn't make it quite as far as her eyes. She was getting tense, as was everyone in the bar.

Krystal had started to talk about calling the local hospitals, her instinct for melodrama kicking in. "It will kill Mom if something's happened to him. It's the only explanation for him being this late."

And then suddenly, there he was, the Paul Newman eyes glowing as he apologized. The traffic was terrible. He'd forgotten to recharge his cell. There'd been a contract crisis with one of his clients—brilliant singer, the whole world would hear about her very soon. The lines flowed smooth and easy from his mouth, as if he'd said them a thousand times before, as if he didn't even have to think about injecting a note of sincerity.

Mom turned to Nate. "See?"

What Nate saw was what he knew—a cheat, a scammer and a sleaze who happened to have the same eyes as one of the world's all-time sexiest men. "Mom, we need to talk," he said.

"Not now, honey, for heck's sake."

"Yes, now." He should have said it all right away. Deep down, he'd been half hoping that the guy just wouldn't show, and it would all be a moot point. No such luck.

He turned to Cole, aware of Lannie standing there, stranded in her role as his date. A part of him expected her to bail, and a part of him *wanted* her to, so that he didn't have to start on the apologies and explanations and histories.

"Cole, I stumbled across a couple of your other names. There's Mickinder, McHinder and Mitchlinder, so far. Which one exactly are you offering to my mother tomorrow?"

"Business names," Cole answered, without blinking an eye. "Mickinder is my legal name for documentation. It's hard to spell. It was originally Czech, two generations ago, but it's been Americanized. I'm not responsible if people get it wrong sometimes."

"So you keep Cale McHinder and Kyle Mitchlinder just for debts?"

"Listen, I've had some disappointments." The blue eyes had gone cold. "Your mother knows that. A business partner ratted on me a few years ago and put me deep in the hole. Another time, I trusted a handshake deal when I shouldn't have. Things like that haunt a man even after he's moved on." He turned to Nate's mother and notched up the charm. "Have I ever been dishonest with you, Belle?"

"No, no, you haven't, sweetheart. Nate, don't do this."

"Who else is going to do it, Mom? Who else ever truly has

your best interests at heart, apart from me? And yet you'll never, ever believe it and you never, ever listen."

"You're embarrassing the—"

"Embarrassing? Let me tell you about embarrassing. I am embarrassed to my very soul by having to deal with your mess, time after time. Do you remember the year you bought Krystal a pony that you couldn't afford, when she was thirteen, and you had him stabled at that barn?"

"She wanted a pony so much!"

"And you couldn't pay the stabling fees one month, because you'd moved and had to cover the security deposit on the new apartment, so you just pretended it wasn't happening and never went back there to take care of him? Remember that?"

"Nate, it's so long ago!"

"Do you know how I felt when I finally found out about it, and had to show up at the barn after three months, and apologize on your behalf, and pay the back fees and feed bills, and arrange to have the poor pony sold, and hear about how he didn't get fed for four days until the barn owners realized you weren't showing up to take care of him?"

Okay, Nate, stop.

He didn't know why he'd picked that one tiny incident, out of all the others he could have chosen. The Reverend Beale had heard. Lannie had heard. He visibly had to press his lips together to stop himself from telling other stories, similarly pathetic stories of dropped responsibilities and petty debts and poor judgement.

He felt the brush of Lannie's hand on his arm. "Let me get that meal served out."

"No," said his mother, "We're going ahead with the rehearsal first."

So they did, and that was…kind of pathetic, too, because at least half of tomorrow's wedding guests were here. They received an unintentional preview of Mom's plan to enter from behind the bar and wind between the tables, dropping a flower in front of each female guest. They listened to the tinny recording of her bridal entrance music, "At Long Last Love," written by a different Cole and sung by another man with legend-status blue eyes.

Clever, but it would fall flat tomorrow, now that everyone had already heard it.

"Spoiler alert," Lannie murmured drily in his hearing, and he shot her a suffering look. "Sorry," she said, wincing.

"No, it's an appropriate comment." As well as another nail in the coffin of his dark mood.

He'd known he had to bring Lannie to meet his family in order for the two of them to work out if there was a chance in hell of their staying together. A wedding should have been the right opportunity—an organized, joyful occasion, everyone dressed up and on their best behavior. He should have realized it would never work out that way with Mom involved.

Weddings. The best and the worst.

"I'm going to talk to the chef," Lannie said. "Make sure he has service ready the moment they're done with the rehearsal. That'll—" she waved her hands "—distract the guests."

From the element of farce and fiasco, Nate understood.

"Then I'm going to go sit in that place across the street for a while," Lannie added. She studied his face, as if looking for confirmation.

"Go," he said, adding with more bluntness and bitterness than he'd meant to, "If you can't stand it."

"Sheesh, Nate, not because *I* can't stand it," she answered angrily, and he didn't have time to work out what she meant, because it turned out they had to do the winding between the tables part again, because Mom had forgotten that she planned to walk down her crooked equivalent of an aisle on Nate's arm.

By the time the rehearsal was finished, Lannie had done as

she'd said she would and disappeared out the front door. He was deeply relieved that she wasn't here, and yet he blamed her for it, too.

She did this all the time.

She just opted out.

It was weak, wasn't it? It was wrong.

Belle's bar was never going to be a success, as things currently stood.

Seated at a pavement table right out front, at the place across the street, Lannie detailed the problems in her head as if preparing a formal business plan. Amateurish decor. Outdated menu. Stage area for the singers taking up too much valuable space for too little return. No pavement tables to take advantage of the mild San Diego climate. No harmony between the various elements. No clear branding. The biggest issue was that they were in direct competition with this far more inviting establishment, whose owners obviously had a lot more money to invest and a lot more business flair.

Her meal and drink arrived. Soup, a bread roll and soda water. Her stomach felt too queasy to think of anything more substantial.

It wasn't her stomach's fault, it was her heart. She'd left it behind with Nate, in his mother's bar across the street.

Had she done the right thing in leaving him on his own? His whole body language had suggested he was crying out for her to go so that he didn't have to worry about how she was handling things. She could see how much he hated having his family's failings and weaknesses shoved in Lannie's face, and since she couldn't do anything about the failings, she took her face out of there.

He knew where to find her. He would come for her when the whole thing was safely over.

Which wouldn't be for a while.

She finished her own meal and waited, wondering where the rehearsal dinner guests were up to with theirs. Dessert? She didn't want any for herself, but ordered a soothing herbal tea because her tension still wouldn't let her stomach settle.

Nate appeared, and for a moment her heart lifted like a bird. Her emotions had been so volatile ever since Mom and Dad's visit upstate.

But the uplift didn't last. This was Cole coming out with Nate, and the mood between them wasn't pretty.

She saw everything as it happened, and heard some of it. They were locked in an ugly argument. Nate tried to keep it subtle, but Cole seemed to want the whole world to know. Every time Nate brought up another damning fact, Cole brazened it out, acted like the injured party, offered smooth or indignant explanations. Belle appeared, begging both of them to stop. Lannie would have gone across and begged with her, except she was so sure Nate wouldn't want that from her.

Had he seen her sitting here?

Should she pretend she wasn't watching?

It all ended soon after Belle's appearance. Cole turned his anger on his fiancée and reduced her to tears, berating her about her son's ingratitude, telling her not to come over to his apartment tonight as planned—Belle had wanted to talk through the final arrangements for tomorrow—because he needed some space.

He strode off, and Belle was visibly torn. Follow, or stay with Nate? And who should she be angry with?

She chose Nate, letting fly with a barrage of emotional, reckless language, and Lannie knew why.

Nate was *safe,* because he truly cared.

At some level, Belle knew that she could say anything, do anything, and still Nate would always be there for her. He would forgive her, step in to deal with her problems, pay her debts, swallow his impatience and anger and just do it.

Over and over again.

It said a huge amount about his character, and Lannie loved him for it. Oh, and she needed to tell him so, because it was time he knew. But it wasn't good for him, all this endless forgiveness and responsibility for his family, and it wasn't good for her to watch him doing it. She could see how it had shaped him, made him too intolerant and unyielding too often, robbed him of optimism and trust. She could see, too, how it would drag him down for the rest of his life if he didn't find a way to loosen the chains.

Okay, Belle was done. She stood there glaring at her son, with her arms folded across the front of her brightly colored top. In disbelief, Lannie saw him reach into his back pocket, bring out his wallet and hand over a wad of bills. She heard a handful of his words. "...should cover the hair appointments and the flowers for tomorrow."

His mother had just yelled at him on a sidewalk in front of half of San Diego and now she expected *money?*

Apparently it wasn't necessary to thank him for it, either. Belle stuffed the notes into her purse, whirled around and went back into the bar, leaving Nate on the pavement, his whole body vibrating with the mix of anger and love and hopeless frustration that Lannie had begun to understand was so damaging to him.

He looked across the street and saw her, apparently for the first time since he'd emerged from the bar. He'd glanced in this direction once or twice during the exchanges with Cole and Belle, but Lannie guessed he'd been too immersed in the conflict to find her amongst the Friday night crowd. She waved at him and he set off across the street. Leaving cash on the table for the check, she stood and went to meet him, with a pointless need to save him the extra energy after he'd expended so much on dealing with Belle and Cole tonight.

They met up on the sidewalk and she was shocked at the

expression in his eyes, a cold simmering rage that she'd never seen there before. It wasn't directed at her, she understood that completely, but the fact that he could look this way at all really scared her. He was being eaten up inside—by anger, by powerlessness, by love that couldn't do any good—and the damage was taking its toll.

"You have to let go, Nate," she told him urgently, too upset to choose her moment. "You just have to get out of their lives if it affects you like this."

"Just get out of their lives?" he echoed, his voice almost without expression.

"Yes! Stop solving things, stop giving them money, stop telling them things they, for whatever reason, aren't able to hear. Just get out while you can."

"Is that what you'd do? You'd get out?"

"I— This isn't about me. This is about watching you grappling with Cole, trying to tell your mother things out of love that she reacts to as if you were beating her. This is about your *face,* Nate. Your eyes."

"They're my family. You think I should just drop them stone cold?"

"Don't put words into my mouth that I haven't said."

He ignored her. "What would happen if I wasn't around? My mother would be on the streets."

"Or else she'd have to pick herself up and develop some responsibility. You're *enabling* her, like buying alcohol for a chronic drunk."

"Can you spare me the pop psychology? That is an appalling comparison. You met them *yesterday,* for heck's sake, and you think you know more about the situation than I do when I've been in it my whole life."

"Sometimes we can see clearest when the impressions are fresh. Your family is damaging you very badly, Nate."

"I'm the successful one. I think the damage lies elsewhere."

Well, he'd inherited one thing from his mother, Lannie decided—the inability to hear wise advice. He was striding along the busy sidewalk, ignoring her difficulty in keeping up.

"Can you really be so lightweight?" he suddenly demanded. "So clueless about responsibility? I guess you can. You've never had to follow anything through. There's always been a way out for you."

"Do you think I don't know how lucky I am? Lightweight and clueless? That is *unforgivably* unfair. My whole adult life I've tried to be aware of my good fortune and not let it blind me. I've tried to make responsible choices and find my own way and, yes, I've bailed out a couple of times when I've been really sure it was the right thing to do."

"Walking out of a restaurant—"

She didn't listen to his interruption. "Pig-headedly pushing ahead with the consequences of a mistake or a stupid choice is apparently the mature thing to do, according to you. I think you're totally wrong."

"—because a couple of guys were getting rowdy was *a responsible choice* and *the right thing to do.* Boy, your life takes place on a level of earth-shattering importance, doesn't it?"

"You're never going to let me forget that, are you? One hissy fit, one wasted dessert, one decision that the effort wasn't worth it, and it just can't be allowed to die."

"I think you should live my life for a little longer before you're so convinced you know spit about any of this."

Were *they* fighting now?

Was this their first major fight?

She had to blink back tears, hating the fact that she was feeling so much love for him and he wasn't in the mood to hear about it. Hating that things could be so good between them in so many ways, but there was this block in understanding, this anger, this difference in the way they saw things and handled things, and it seemed to loom larger every minute.

"I don't want to say anything more. I don't want things to come out that I won't be able to take back and that we won't ever forget," she whispered, close to tears.

"Me, neither. I don't want that, either. Hell, I really, really don't!"

They walked all the way back to the hotel without another word, and then in the elevator, when she wasn't expecting it at all, he suddenly turned to her, crushed her in his arms and told her, "I love you. I *love* you."

"I love you, too," she whispered in answer. "So much." But then she didn't know what to say next, and apparently neither did he.

Chapter Nineteen

I love you wasn't enough.

Nate had known half his life or longer that love wasn't enough. If love was enough, then his mother and sister would be fine, happy, settled. If love was enough, then the things he did for them would have the power to change their lives. If love was enough, they'd listen to him sometimes.

I love you was only the beginning.

When he said it to Lannie and she said it back to him, it felt like the most powerful thing in the world, but it was just the start, it wasn't the answer.

The elevator pinged its announcement of their arrival on the seventh floor while he still had her crushed in his arms and before he'd said any of the other words that burned in him to be spoken. *Thank you* and *I'm sorry* were the most important.

Did she understand how much he hated the imprisonment in his own anger that always came after a difficult time with his family? Did she understand that he said things the wrong way, to the wrong person? He'd wanted to yell at Krystal and Mom, but he was worn out from dealing with their lives, so instead he'd yelled at Lannie.

Why was she still here? Why hadn't she just bailed? Didn't she always bail?

He held her hand as they walked along the corridor, bent to kiss her because he knew he couldn't go another step without feeling the touch of her mouth against his. He wanted to talk about tonight—the disaster of Cole, his mother's inability to listen, Krystal's addiction to emotional drama—but the words were locked inside him and he was afraid of what might happen if he let them out.

"Will she go through with the wedding?" Lannie asked, as he slid the keycard into the slot outside their room.

"She has every intention to."

"Would Krystal try to talk her out of it?"

"Krystal enjoys this. It's like living in a soap opera, for her. Or an episode of *Cops*," he added grimly, thinking again of what he'd learned about Cole's shady past.

"Do you want to sit in the bar downstairs for a while to unwind?"

She was trying to help, trying to unlock his anger and ease it away, but he couldn't take that from her. Not tonight. "I think I'll just take a shower," he said. "You must be pretty tired. I am. It's ten o'clock—one in the morning, New York time—and we were up at five."

Had she gotten the hint? He didn't trust himself to make love to her tonight. It would seem tainted by everything that had gone before. It might relax him, but he didn't want to be relaxed that way, and it sure as hell wouldn't relax her. He would feel as if he was using her, using that beautiful body and generous spirit. She was worth so much more than the kind of love-making he had in him right now. She was worth more than making love to her when he feared it might be for the last time, if they couldn't find a way through.

"I'm exhausted," she admitted.

"Get some rest. I'll try not to disturb you when I'm out of the shower."

Belle's wedding day dawned clear and dry with the promise of later heat. Lannie woke early again, surprised at how well she'd slept, and at how her body seemed to want even more. Nate had already gone from the bed. She lay there lazily for another half hour, then showered and dressed and found him downstairs having breakfast. The smell of the coffee hit her nostrils with unpleasant strength. It wasn't the same brand they used at Sheridan Lakes and she didn't like it as much.

"You disappeared," she accused him gently.

"Didn't want to wake you."

"And I was fast asleep before you finished your shower last night. There's no proof you ever came to bed at all." She smiled at him, wanting so much for last night's argument not to matter. If she could show him that she believed in their shared power to move past it, then maybe he'd believe it, too.

He grinned back, a complicated expression, full of love but unwilling, holding something back. He said slowly, "I held you in your sleep for nearly an hour."

Her heart turned over. "Did you?"

"You didn't even stir."

"Krystal is supposed to be picking me up this morning, right? To go get our hair done with the bride? But I'm not sure what time."

"Krystal probably isn't sure, either. She'll call. Eventually." There was a weary, resigned note to his prediction.

"You know how this is going to unfold, don't you?"

"Look," he began, palpably reluctant, "it won't be well

organized. You didn't have to say yes, yesterday, when Mom and Krystal wanted you to be a part of the wedding day preparations."

"Yes, I did. I was touched that they wanted me. It's just one day, Nate, no matter how crazy and chaotic it is."

"True."

The hours passed in a blur of phone calls and changed arrangements, no stops for meals, just sugar and fat filled snacks grabbed on the run—cheap donuts, fizzy cola drinks, salty cheese curls that left Lannie's fingers stained yellow and a metallic taste in her mouth.

For some reason the cleaners who did the bar had been told they weren't required today. "To simplify the schedule," Belle had said. Not one of her best decisions, and then she and Krystal had almost forgotten about it.

The three women had already finished at the hair salon, each with an elaborate up-do kept in place by a helmet of hairspray, when Krystal suddenly gasped, "Shoot, we have to go clean up the bar from last night! I completely forgot!"

Being the bride, Belle was exempted, which left Krystal and Lannie getting down and dirty with their over-complicated hair threatening their balance and risking getting scraped against walls and tables as they swept and wiped and sprayed. Lannie hated the smell of the cleaning products and had to go out to the bar's back alley twice to get some air. She could still taste those horrible cheese curls.

Nate, meanwhile, was helping the chef with the catering, as Belle had only come up with a final tally of guest numbers this morning and they had thirty percent more people than she'd originally thought. "I really don't know how that happened," she said. "But I've tallied it five times."

He caught Lannie for a private moment outside the walk-in refrigerator, looking horrified at her combination of elaborately styled hair, rubber gloves and water-splashed jeans.

She told him, before he could speak, "Don't apologize for this. I'm fine. Everyone's emotions run high on a wedding day, and there's always something that doesn't go to plan. It's why we're here. For your family."

"Yeah, all right." He let out a controlled sigh, and Lannie just wanted to get him away somewhere that would be safe for his suffering spirit.

Impossible, of course.

Because of the cleaning, Krystal and Lannie were two hours late collecting the cake and the flowers. They then had to go back to the bar to put the flowers on the tables, and Lannie needed time to dress. On the way to Belle's apartment, Krystal took a short cut that trapped them in traffic and cost an extra forty minutes. The bride was beside herself by the time they arrived. "I have fifteen minutes to dress!"

But in the end it didn't matter that Belle arrived at her wedding ceremony a half hour late.

The groom never showed.

Lannie thought these must have been the slowest ninety minutes of her life, watching Belle's excitement turn to anxiety, overhearing the failed phone calls—"He's not picking up at his apartment...his cell is switched off"—and running interference with the uneasy guests.

Krystal did her soap opera thing and began calling all the hospitals in the area. Belle began to apologize to everyone—to Reverend Beale, over and over. "Something's happened," she kept saying to people. "Please order drinks from the bar. They're on the house, of course."

Nate eventually drew Belle aside and said in the suffering voice Lannie was starting to know too well, "Mom, he should have been here two hours ago."

"But you know what his work is like. Something urgent could have come up."

"So urgent that he couldn't call you? When he's late for his own wedding?"

She said, faltering and defensive, "Krystal's calling the hospitals."

"I know. She's gone through the whole listing. There's no one been admitted under his name." The word *name* fell awkwardly into the air. Nate had managed not to say "under any of his names." He added, "I think we should tell people not to hang around. And when they've left, we'll drive over to Cole's apartment and see if—I don't know. Just check things out."

Lannie's temples felt as if they had knotted rope tightening around them. She could hardly bear to look at Belle's face, the careful, beautiful make-up gone shiny, smears of black around her eyes where she'd rubbed at them, on the edge of tears. She could have strangled a couple of the guests, making free with the on-the-house alcohol and completely oblivious to Belle's pain.

She felt Nate's complex, painful emotions as if they were happening in her own body—the bitter sense of I-told-you-so, the apprehension about what had actually gone wrong. Maybe Krystal should have been calling the local police stations and lock-ups, not the hospitals.

All she wanted, once again, was to get Nate out of here, back to his beloved mountains where he could breathe, and be his own man. She understood his need for breathing space so much better now. What she didn't understand was how he could keep himself together, keep the love in place, year after year.

Maybe they could leave. If they could sort out what had happened, farewell the guests, close the bar, get Belle safely home, maybe there'd be a late flight…

Surreptitiously she took out her phone, logged onto its Internet connection and started keying in search criteria on the airline sites. She found a red-eye they might just make in time, if this excruciating evening ended soon.

"Everyone is leaving," Nate said, coming up behind her and putting his hands on her shoulders. She disconnected her phone, not wanting him to know just how protective she felt. Had he seen those flight details on the screen? He might hate this worse than anything—the thought that she felt a need to rescue him.

"I'm glad," she answered quickly. "For your mother's sake. He's not going to show, is he?"

"I don't think so."

"Do you have any idea what could have happened?"

"Couple of theories." He didn't elaborate, adding only, "I'm taking her over to his apartment as soon as she's said her goodbyes."

Belle had switched into hostess mode, as the guests began to melt away, her performance poignantly brave. "Thank you so much for coming… It was so good of you to be here. I know Cole would appreciate it… I'll let you know what's happening the moment we have some news."

It was pretty clear what had happened as soon as they stepped inside Cole's apartment, using Belle's key. Krystal had tried to have her mother stay behind, but Belle had insisted on coming and Nate had agreed. "Let her see for herself, Krys," he'd muttered to his sister, as if he'd already known what the four of them would find.

The apartment was empty.

Not especially clean, with piled trash bags still sitting in the middle of the floor in each room, but empty.

They all took in the echoing spaces in miserable silence. Belle looked older, suddenly, and Lannie wanted to put her arms around Nate's mother and hug her, but Krystal was already there, delivering curse words that condemned the vanished groom beyond the grave and back to the cradle. "I hope he rots in hell, the b—"

"What's he left you with, Mom? What's he saddled you with?" Nate asked, his voice little more than a rasp.

"Just some clothes, at my place."

"I mean, what liabilities? The liquor license is in joint names, I noticed. That's…probably a good thing. What about the lease?"

"Just mine."

"How much do you owe?"

"We need to pay all our suppliers next week. We're already a little overdue."

"Do you have it?"

"No."

"And is that all? Just the suppliers?"

"I—I don't know. Cole was keeping tabs on all that."

"I just bet he was."

Tabs and sleazy fingers.

"My portfolio!" Krystal said, on a wail. She was only twenty-two, twelve years younger than Nate, Lannie reminded herself. "My style consultant!"

"How much did you give him?" Nate asked his half sister.

"Two thousand dollars."

"Where did you get it?"

"I borrowed it from a friend. She needs it back by the end of the month for a down payment on a car. And I promised her—I thought—Cole said—"

Under his breath, Nate swore. "I scared him off," he muttered. "I confronted him, and he ran." Was he implying that Belle and Krystal would have been better off if the wedding had actually gone ahead, Lannie wondered?

He said out loud, "We'll manage something."

"Could we meet for coffee at your hotel tomorrow morning,

Nate?" Krystal said in appeal. "Put our heads together and come up with a strategy?"

"Sure."

He'd just agreed to coffee with Krystal tomorrow morning, while tonight's red-eye departed at ten-twenty. Lannie looked at her watch. There was no way they'd make that flight now, anyhow. They were here in the middle of the fall-out, and they'd have to stay as planned.

Belle blinked hard several times, then clapped her hands together briskly. "Well. We can't stand here all night, looking at this mess."

"I'll stay over with you tonight at your place, Mom, okay?" Krystal offered, her sympathy a little cloying despite its sincerity.

"I'd like that, honey." She didn't mention the honeymoon hotel, already paid for, but added abruptly, "I think I knew. At heart. He filled my head with such wonderful plans. Singing in my own bar, my own repertoire, no one else to answer to. And Krystal getting her big break with his Hollywood connections. But deep down I knew. It was all too good to be true."

Lannie saw Nate fighting not to speak, not to yell at her, out of half a lifetime of pent-up frustration, *It's always too good to be true, Mom* or *If you knew, why did you go along with it?* She felt a flood of shattering weariness flood over her, making her feel sick to her stomach. She would have loved to have taken that flight, just to be out of here.

Away.

Free.

Untouched by the sadness and mess.

But she was stuck. And it was her heart that made her stuck. And her heart was stubborn at the worst of times—stubbornly in love with Nate, while watching all the freedom and life and generous love he had in him being slowly strangled by a mother and sister who didn't deserve everything he kept trying to give.

Chapter Twenty

Lannie knew she had to leave the waterfront and get back to the hotel. She'd been gone too long already. Their flight left in a few hours and they still needed to check out and say goodbye to Nate's family.

In their room, she found Nate packing. "Not as neat as you, I expect, with the dresses and shoes," he said, as if everything was normal.

"It's fine. I'll sort it out back home."

"You had those shoe bags…"

"Yes, did you use them?"

"Figured you didn't want dirt from the soles getting on your dress fabric."

"Thanks. But please let me finish now."

Suddenly they both dropped the pretense. Nate stood in the middle of the room and faced her down and she couldn't scurry off to the bathroom, the way she wanted, to pack up her make-up and toiletries. "I was getting worried about you, Lannie."

"I know. That's why I came back."

"You mean you would have stayed out longer? Where were you? I wanted to come looking. You didn't take your cell with you."

"The waterfront."

"That's the first place I would have looked."

They managed a tentative smile at each other. Some things between them were still good, still right. Some understanding was still in place. The tension in the room released a little.

"How's your nausea?" he asked.

"Much better. I expect it'll come and go, won't it?"

He gave no answer to this. There was too much to say and no way to say it. Or else there was nothing to say, because as soon as they tried they would start getting it wrong.

It didn't take them long to finish packing and check out. There was a line of cabs waiting in the curved driveway in the side street beside the hotel, and they took the first one, and had the driver wait for them when they reached Belle's bar.

Inside, they found her cleaning on her own, since the cleaners hadn't turned up. Nothing had been done last night, and there were dirty plates and glasses piled high in the kitchen. There'd been no actual wedding, but the wedding guests had still given themselves a great time. Belle didn't seem able to distinguish between freeloaders and genuine friends, and Lannie knew it was another of the issues that drove Nate crazy.

"Krystal's not here helping?" he asked his mother.

Belle straightened and leaned on her broom. "She deserved a break."

"You shouldn't treat her that way, Mom, she's an adult."

"She's twenty-two. She's a baby. I have that list of checks you're going to write for me, Natey, with the amounts and the names. It—it comes to a little more than I thought it would. I hope that's okay."

"I said I'd cover them, Mom. If necessary, I can take out a loan. My credit's good."

"You're wonderful."

"Call me the second there's a problem, okay? Don't wait until your back is to the wall before I hear about it."

"I won't. My back isn't going to be to the wall. I've learned something this time!"

"That's good. That's great." He didn't believe it, Lannie could tell.

The three of them talked for a little, but it was awkward, too many difficult subjects that no one wanted to go near.

"Well, we have the cab waiting outside," Nate finally said, triggering a round of emotional goodbyes.

Lannie was close to tears, not knowing if she'd ever meet this flawed, warm-spirited woman again, yet feeling as if she'd already taken Belle to her heart. Belle seemed to feel the same way, judging by the strength of her hug. It was a nice moment, one thing that was right in a whole sea of things that weren't.

Back in the cab on the way to the airport, Nate asked, "So… what would you do?"

"About the bar? If I were you?"

"Yes."

"I wouldn't just write checks, Nate."

"Yeah, I had that impression. So? Instead?"

"Take over the lease, put in a manager I could trust, do a professional refit that actually works. The refit would pay for itself pretty fast by bringing more people in. I'd have your mom work shifts at the bar to start with, for a percentage of the profits, so that she had a stake in its success but not too much responsibility or control."

"You've thought it all out."

"I have. I kind of…couldn't help myself."

"I know how that is."

"She's good with people. There's no reason the place couldn't turn a profit if it was run realistically, not as a fantasy, with the singing. Friday and Saturday nights she could sing if she wanted, if the turnover was enough to pay for someone else to tend bar. That is—I never heard her sing. Is she good?"

"She is. Not great. But good. Singing in a place like that would suit her range."

"You could see how the singing panned out, if it brought people in or kept them away. No actual stage area, because you lose too many tables that way, and the stage area they've put in is *ugly*. She could sit on a stool with a hand-held mike. If she puts in the hard yards and the bar turns enough of a profit, eventually she might take a bigger percentage, or take the lease back into her own name."

"Treat her like a child, in other words, making her earn her privileges. Assuming she'd even let me do it that way. She has a long, long history of never taking my advice."

"Don't you think you already treat her like a child, Nate? You rescue her from all her mistakes, never make her deal with the consequences on her own. *Make* her take your advice, by spelling out to her that it's sink or swim. She does it the way you want, or you pull the plug. Mean it, and don't back down. You take everything on your own shoulders. With Krystal it's even worse, because your mom lets her off the hook all the time, the way she did just now, not wanting her to come in and clean, so your sister knows she has two people constantly at the ready to bail her out, one with emotional support and the other with money."

She waited for him to say something about the ways she'd been let off the hook herself—the broken engagement, the uncompleted MBA. He stayed silent, but she felt his thoughts.

It was *wrong*.

They had to deal with this. He had to listen to her, and she had to say it right, hard and steady and strong, even when she felt more like crying.

"Before you say it," she told him, "When I bailed out of my wedding and my degree, I was by no means off the hook. I wasn't ducking my responsibilities. I went and saw all my professors and explained my reasons, all by myself, dealt with their disappointment and attempts to talk me round, face-to-face. I phoned every wedding guest personally, even the ones who'd only been invited as business associates of my father. I returned all the engagement gifts and wedding gifts that some people had sent in advance, paid my parents back for everything they'd spent, handled weeks…months…of Walton telling me he didn't understand, in texts and emails and phone calls and horrible confrontations."

"I don't want to talk about the past. I want to talk about the future."

"We have to talk about the past, because the past is what's getting in the way. For both of us." She hated that she kept coming so close to tears. Hated, too, that in the struggle to fight the tears she probably sounded way too harsh and hard-edged.

But it was impossible to keep talking now. They'd reached the set-down area in front of the departure concourse, and they'd cut the timing pretty fine. They almost had to run. By the time they reached the gate, the flight was already boarding. There were some conversations you just couldn't have on a crowded airplane, with the drone of the engines a constant in the background and attentive business-class flight attendants moving up and down the aisles.

Still, they tried.

"I asked you to marry me four hours ago," Nate said. "And you didn't even want to hear the words, because you were trying—you're still trying—to pretend as much as possible that this isn't even happening."

"That's not true. That's not why I didn't want to hear it."

"And last night, I saw you checking flight schedules."

"For you, not for me. For both of us. I wasn't just going to run out on you."

"But that's what you want to do now. You're having my baby and you're planning to shut me out. You can't do it. I'm the father. No matter what happens between us, I have the legal right to be involved."

"I know that, Nate. As for the marriage proposal, do you really think I wanted to hear it that way? To hear you say it out of desperation and that crippling sense of responsibility you always have? Do you really think a marriage agreed on in that spirit would have a fair chance of surviving? This is the twenty-first century. I don't *need* your ring and your name."

"I guess you don't." Silence. "Are you saying it's over, Lannie?"

"I won't be another millstone around your neck, along with your mother and sister, to complete the set. I won't. And until you can find a way to change that, until we can do this with love and freedom and joy, not just the weight of your crippling sense of responsibility, which is *killing* you and changing you and making you take your anger out on me for things I haven't done and don't deserve—then I think we're stuck." Her voice fogged with tears and she hated her own weakness.

"Stuck? You? Has to be a first."

"Yes, Nate, believe it or not, I don't see a way of bailing out of this one."

"You didn't answer my question, just now. Are you saying it's over?"

"Yes." Don't cry, don't cry, don't cry. With an iron will, the same kind of will she'd needed during those hours on the slopes of Mount Ararat, she forced the tears back, made her voice come out clearly. "I think that's what I'm saying."

"We have a problem," Nate heard from one of his senior staff on Monday morning, within three minutes of arriving back at the hotel.

He and Lannie had taken his car from the airport, having left it in the long-stay parking lot for the four nights they'd spent away. The overnight flight home had left them both tired and wrung out, and she hadn't argued when he'd dropped her directly in front of her cabin and told her to rest.

He could feel his own downbeat state of mind like a fog around them both, all the powerless love and anger and hopelessness he felt about Krystal and Mom, all the ways, most of them unfair, that he was off-loading it onto Lannie. She'd been right about that, he could see.

He *knew* she wasn't like his family in so many important ways, but his jaded perspective was a visceral, illogical thing that he couldn't talk himself out of, right now.

It was over between them.

She was having his baby, but she'd said it was over and he couldn't find a reason to argue, because in so many ways she was right.

"Tell me," he said, in answer to his staffer.

"We're double-booked for the weekend. Two wedding parties, both expecting to use the bridal marquee on the southern lawn."

"That's impossible!"

"Unfortunately, it's happened. One of the couples had a fight and broke off the wedding. The bride called to cancel verbally. She was supposed to follow it up in writing, but she never did. The two of them made it up, the wedding was back on and because she'd only called and not cancelled in writing, she correctly believed that her reservation for the reception should still stand. Meanwhile, someone—we can't work out who—acted on the verbal cancellation and when another couple wanted the same date, it showed in our system as being available."

"Nobody noticed when the advance payments came in? When the arrangements for numbers and catering and all of that were made?"

"Different people handled different elements."

"So we're screwed."

"I thought you'd want to be the one to work out what we can do."

"You thought right." He swung into action, checking guest numbers and menus, looking at staff availability and timing.

One wedding was quite a bit larger than the other, the second reception was scheduled to begin an hour later than the first. For the smaller event, the couple were using a wedding planner he'd worked with before, and whom he knew could be relied on to talk sense into over-the-top brides, if this one turned out to fall into that category.

He navigated his way through several extremely delicate, difficult phone calls and by the end of the day, both couples had agreed to consider his proposed solution and get back to him with a final decision by tomorrow lunch time.

The bride with the larger wedding had been a complete witch about it and wouldn't agree to the tiniest change of menu or timing. The bride with the smaller guest list had listened to everything he'd said and compromised cheerfully wherever she could. All she wanted was a little time to talk everything over with her groom.

Meanwhile, he hadn't seen Lannie all day.

She called him at seven, asking if they could eat dinner together in her cabin, but there was no way. The double-booked weddings had taken most of his day, and he had a hundred other tasks to catch up on tonight, as well as writing out all those overdue checks for his mother so he could mail them first thing in the morning.

"I'm sorry," he said. "I can't."

But the sound of her voice on the phone made the strength drain from his legs and if she'd pushed, he would have thrown his responsibilities to the four winds and appeared at her front door in a heartbeat. He had to grit his teeth and remind himself how quickly everything could spiral out of control in this business if you ever let yourself drop the ball.

But, oh, if she pushed just a little bit…

She didn't push. "Okay, then, I'll sum it up now." Her voice had turned brisk, as sudden as a weather change in the fall. "I researched local OB/GYN specialists today, and made an appointment for a checkup next Monday at ten. If you're available and want to come, that would be great."

"So you're planning to stay in the area?"

"Do you want me to leave?"

"No. I'm just…"

"Surprised," she finished for him.

"Yes."

Silence. A sigh. "Anyhow…no need to give me a decision now. I'm just telling you about the appointment in case you want to be there."

"Of course I want to be there!"

"And yet somehow you're still surprised that I'm planning to stay in the area. Your commitment I'm supposed to take for granted, while you immediately expect me to cut and run." Her voice changed suddenly, went ragged at the edges. "Nate, I can't do this right now. I'm sorry. I can't."

He heard the sound of the phone disconnecting, thought about calling her back but knew it wouldn't help. Yesterday, she'd left their hotel room for over an hour to go walking on the San Diego waterfront.

Bailing out, he'd thought.

Bailing *again*.

But maybe she'd been right to want the space. Maybe space was the only thing that could possibly work in their favour, right now. Maybe it wasn't always a matter of bailing.

He thought about the one time in his life when he'd chosen space over responsibility—the time he'd come east after his fight with Mom twelve years ago, and had decided to stay. He hadn't considered that to be bailing out. He'd been there for his mother and sister in every way they needed, other than his day-to-day presence. They'd had his checks in the mail, his support over the phone. He knew these mountains had been an escape, a necessary distance, and they'd saved him.

Escape…responsibility…distance…saving yourself…bailing out.

The boundaries were blurred. The angles were different. He couldn't work it out.

Maybe Lannie was right, he thought once more.

Space. He would give both of them some space this week, and maybe by her appointment next Monday, he'd know for sure. He checked his electronic planner, found that he was already free, and added in OB/GYN, not sure if he would be there for her purely as the father of her coming child, or as the man who loved her and might one day win her whole heart.

Chapter Twenty-One

"Weddings," Nate had said to Lannie in early June. "They bring out the best and the worst."

It was true, she decided as she stood in the restaurant kitchen, and the truth of it was on show tonight at Sheridan Lakes.

Out in the huge, beautiful marquee on the southern lawn, they had a bridezilla who hadn't compromised one inch on her plans all week, even though she was the one who'd cancelled over the phone, failed to follow up, and thereby initiated this whole mess in the first place.

Inside, in their flagship restaurant Lavande, which had been hastily reconfigured to squeeze in eight more tables, they had a generous, pretty bride who'd told Lannie a half hour earlier, "I hope this hasn't given the whole hotel a horrible week. You look a little tired…"

"Oh, I'm fine," she'd said, pasting on a big smile.

But it wasn't true.

She wasn't fine.

She was wearing the pinky-gold dress she'd brought to San Diego for Belle's wedding, but it didn't make her feel beautiful tonight. The matching shoes—footwear equivalent of a thong bikini—murdered her feet.

She felt tired down to the marrow of her bones, having put aside her work on the wilderness packages for the past two days in order to ensure that the beyond-capacity guest list at the hotel was fully catered for and the two lavish wedding receptions ran smoothly.

It wasn't the work that had tired her out, though.

It wasn't even the baby growing inside her, becoming more precious to her heart every day, changing her body and her emotions faster than she could handle.

It was losing Nate.

She'd barely seen him since he'd dropped her at her cabin door on Monday morning, and she missed him with a sense of loss that was physical and emotional and painful and horribly real.

Lannie, you were the one who did this, she told herself. You were the one who told him it was over.

Only because he'd given her no choice.

Only because she knew they would never be able to make a relationship work, let alone a marriage, if he never trusted her commitment and her staying power. If at some level he was always waiting for her to bail. If maybe he was right to expect her to bail, because she still hadn't worked out what she wanted, and who she was. And, too, if she had to stand by and watch him enabling his mother and sister's dependencies and fantasies and impossible plans as he grew more and more angry and locked in his own conflicting feelings for them with every passing year.

How could that work?

It couldn't.

She'd lost Nate, but she'd had no choice. She'd done the only thing possible.

And yet she couldn't believe how different it felt to ending her engagement to Walton. That, too, had been the only thing possible, and it had felt like a liberation, a dizzying burst of new freedom that she'd relished for months.

This was the opposite.

It felt like prison. It made her bones heavier and her body ache. It made even the co-operative bride's wedding feel like a mockery.

"Did you eat tonight?" Nate suddenly appeared beside her. He must have been watching her without her seeing him, she realized—watching her give in to the fatigue and the anguish inside her.

"I'm not hungry," she said.

The chef was putting the finishing touches to a cake he'd baked himself, this time, instead of outsourcing it, and Lannie had been checking to make sure it was perfect, which it was. Two waiters stood by to wheel the cake into the restaurant.

"We had twenty-eight meals that didn't go out to the marquee. Big Bride had her numbers wrong. Go get some salmon and steak."

"And we have appetizers left over from Little Bride," one of the waiters chipped in. They'd been identifying the two women this way all week, based on the size of their respective weddings.

"There you are," Nate said to Lannie, "there's handmade mushroom ravioli, as well."

But she barely heard him, her attention suddenly focused elsewhere...

"Cake's ready to go," the chef said, and the waiters swung into action.

Something wasn't right in her body. She felt a gush of warm fluid...blood, it could only be blood...between her upper thighs. The blood hadn't yet made it onto the floor but it soon would, if she didn't take action.

Blood. Why was she bleeding? It couldn't be good. It had to be very, very bad.

She squeezed her legs together and began to shake, clutching Nate's arm without thinking.

"What's wrong?"

"I'm bleeding."

"Where?" He swore. "You mean—?"

"Yes."

"When did it—?"

"Now. Right now. This second. A—a gush." She wanted to lie down right there on the floor and put her legs in the air, force the blood back, as if gravity had any power whatsoever in this situation.

Nate was urging the same thing. "Lie down. Find the nearest place to lie down."

"The hospital. Take me to the hospital." She gripped his arms, almost fell against him.

"Yes." He swore again. "Yes." He whipped his head around. "Michel, I have to leave. We have an emergency here. Tell Jay to—" He issued a rapid-fire list of instructions and Chef Michel Saint-Gilles nodded, told him there was nothing to worry about at this end, and didn't ask any questions.

Nate made Lannie lean on his arm all the way out the back corridors of the hotel and out to his car, even though she didn't think leaning would do any good. He'd said, "Ambulance?" but she thought there was nothing the paramedics could do en route, and she would reach the hospital ER more quickly in the car.

"You think you're losing it?" he asked.

"I—I must be." They'd grabbed a couple of clean white hotel towels on their way past the linen store and she had one pressed between her legs. "There was blood all down my legs, by the time we had the towels. It's all over my dress."

She didn't know if the bleeding had stopped. There was no cramping. Was that good?

She had no idea. She hadn't even met her obstetrician, yet.

All she knew was that she didn't want this to be happening. She was *desperate* for it not to be happening, which seemed… impossible…when a week ago she hadn't even known there was a baby at all.

Nate drove faster than he should have done, but he knew this road so well, she wasn't afraid on that score. They reached the hospital within half an hour, and she was shown to a private cubicle fifteen minutes after that, discarding the gorgeous dress for a floral cotton hospital gown.

"If you're losing the baby, there's not a lot we can do," a nurse told them, gently matter-of-fact.

"What will happen? I mean, I'll do anything I need to. Bed rest for the whole pregnancy. I don't care. Whatever it takes." The words came all by themselves, spilling out of her with the force of this impossible desperation, this powerful connection she'd made with the idea of a child.

Nate's child.

"We'll have someone down from the maternity department to examine you as soon as we can, and go from there. How much blood have you lost?"

Lannie showed her the towel and the staining on her skin and clothes.

"Mmm," the nurse said. "It's hard to tell."

She left them alone, Lannie on the gurney with her legs raised by a pillow, Nate beside her, his chair pulled up close, stained dress in a slippery plastic bag. He didn't speak, and she wanted him to, so badly, even though she didn't know what she wanted him to say.

"I've barely seen you this week," she said, after several minutes of near-silence. The words seemed thin and inadequate, but she didn't know how else to begin.

"I know," he said, his voice low. "I decided to take a leaf out of your book, try some space, see if it helped."

"Did it?"

He answered her question with one of his own. "What you said just now, that you'd do anything not to lose this baby, do you mean that?"

"It doesn't make sense, does it? You'd have thought this was the obvious way out, right?" She couldn't help sounding bitter and mocking about it.

Mocking him.

Mocking herself.

Mocking the ways they didn't see eye to eye.

Mocking what he thought of her.

"But it isn't?"

"No, it isn't. It sooo isn't!"

"Ah, hell…" he whispered miserably.

After they'd been silent for a few minutes more, she said, "What would have happened if I'd said yes to your marriage proposal? You would have been stuck, wouldn't you? For no reason. No baby, to make at least some sense of what we'd done."

"Lannie—" he began, but then the curtain of their cubicle slid aside and someone in green scrubs appeared.

The doctor's examination didn't take long, conducted beneath a drape of sheeting. "Well," the tiny, cheerful redhead said. "Your uterus is the size it should be for this stage of the pregnancy, and your cervix hasn't opened. I can see there's been significant bleeding but it's tapered off now. We'd better do an ultrasound and see what's happening in there."

"You mean there could still be a baby?" Lannie asked.

"I'd say there's a fair chance. I'm not seeing any obvious indication of miscarriage. But let's take a look."

Lannie burst into tears. "I don't know how much to hope, now."

"Same here," Nate said, his voice choked.

"Wait a little," the doctor said gently. "Take it easy. We're quiet tonight. Should be able to get you along to Imaging within the next half hour." She slid Lannie's notes back into the holder attached to the end of the gurney, and left, slipping through the gap in the curtain.

Nate slid Lannie's hand into his. She saw that he was crying, too, those dark eyes swimming, tears brimming over his long lashes, his lips pressed together and his shoulders jerking as he tried not to let it happen, because he was a man, the strong one, and had been his whole life.

They clung to each other without words, just held on as if this was the end of the world, or the beginning of heaven, they didn't know which, but somehow they had to go through it together, whichever it was. There was no other choice, and Lannie didn't want there to be. He kissed her hair, her wet eyes, her trembling mouth, and she kissed him back, pressed her face against his and felt how warm he was, felt the hardness of his cheekbone and the strength of his jaw.

"Marry me anyway," he said. "This is crazy. It's crazy to think we can't work this out. None of it matters. I love you too much. It couldn't hurt like this if I didn't. It's *real*, it's—I *love* you."

"I love you, too. I don't know what it means. But I love you, and if you weren't here right now, I think I'd die."

"Ah, Lannie… How can I let you *have* a baby or *lose* a baby without me? How can I let you do anything without me, ever again?"

"Just like that, Nate? Marry you just like that?" She was

laughing through her tears. Was this the Nathan Ridgeway she knew? They still had a lot to work through.

"Isn't that how you've always done things? Just like that." He snapped his fingers.

"No! You see!" She struggled to sit a little higher in the gurney, but he reached for her immediately and held her, making her rest back against the pillows. He really wasn't planning on letting her go. "This is the problem, Nate. You were right about the raspberry frangipane tart, okay? I'll give you that one. I shouldn't have bailed that night, when we were having such a great time. We could have ignored those guys, or moved up to the bar. I could have ridden it out. I didn't think it was important at the time, but it was, because it gave you the wrong idea."

"The bar would have been good."

"But when I bail on the big things, it's for a good reason, and you have to see that. Space is important. Time to think is important. Time to work out who you really are and what you want. I didn't want a Harvard MBA. I didn't want to marry the wrong man."

"Definitely don't marry the wrong man…"

"I still don't think I quite know who I am. That's much harder. My parents love me, but—especially Dad—they only see a few possible options. Corporate executive. Society wife. Celebrity spokeswoman for charity. I know there are other choices. I'm fighting to find them. I've been going back and forth for so long, and I still don't know."

"Oh, Lannie, sweetheart, you know! You do know. You're just *you*. You *are* the things you want, the things you do, the things you say. There's no label for it. That's why I love you, because you're impossible to label, impossible to put in a neat little box. You're just Lannie. Perfect, wonderful Lannie. Hell, never doubt that you know who you are!"

"Really?"

"Yes! Why look for a label for yourself, when that's the last thing you want?"

"But my parents—"

"Your parents can deal with it." He buried his face in her hair. "Tell me about last weekend. Tell me why we had it so wrong, that Sunday morning."

"Nate, I didn't want to pretend to you or to myself, that I was immediately ecstatic about having an unplanned pregnancy that I hadn't even suspected until that point, when I didn't know what was going to happen between us, and when I hadn't given myself a second to think through what might be involved."

"You've met Mom and Krystal…"

"Yes. I have. So I know exactly why you're so afraid I'm a flake. I'm not a flake, Nate."

"I know you're not. And you never gave me any real reasons to think that you were. I've seen that this week. And I'm sorry. Hell, I'm so sorry." He pressed his forehead against hers.

"That's not what I really want you to apologize for. That's not the thing that's really wrong."

His body stilled, his hand resting on her hip. He didn't say a word, and she hated feeling him so rigid and fearful, so she went on quickly, "This is the real thing we have to get past, Nate."

"Get past? What thing?"

He sounded so croaky, so near to losing it, and she wanted to tell him *Never mind, it's nothing,* but she knew that would be wrong. They had to deal with this.

"I have been pretty angry with you at times," she said slowly, instead. "You have overcome a million things in your life, a million setbacks and strikes against you. The chaos, and lack of money and serial bad stepfathers, other things, I'm sure, that you haven't told me about. And yet you can't overcome the one thing that's really killing you—your sense of responsibility to people who've blown their chances with you time after time after time. I know you love them. I could love them, too."

"Yeah…?"

"It's not like they're horrible people."

"You don't know how many times I've wished they were. It would be easier to cut off, then."

"I'm not asking you to cut off. Never that. But love isn't always about giving and giving forever, when what you're giving is the wrong thing. You hate the way I've bailed out of things—"

"I don't. Not now that I understand it so much better."

"—but you bail your family out of their problems and mistakes all the time, at huge cost to yourself. Why are you so much harder on yourself than you are on them? I will not be able to stand by and watch it happening, Nate. That's what scares me, the prospect of watching you die inside."

"Can I tell you something?" he asked seriously.

"Please!"

"I talked to Mom for two hours last night on the phone. I did what you did last Sunday, when you disappeared to the waterfront. I've given myself space, this week, and time to think, and I've told her that this was the last time I would give them a free ride. I mailed the checks, so we could start with a clean slate, and we've begun the process of my taking over the bar's lease and liquor license. I'll be looking for a good manager as soon as I can. May have to go out there a couple of times over the next few months."

"Will you stick to it? Will you mean what you've said, next time she or Krystal cycle into a crisis?"

"If it's one thing I know how to do, Lannie, it's sticking to something. And I think they both know I mean it. I couldn't do it when Krystal was still a kid, but you're right, she's a grown woman now, and it's time."

"It is. Oh, I'm so glad you can see it. And I'm going to make you stand your ground over it, Nate."

"I want you to. You're strong. We're strong together. I so want the two of us to be strong together, Lannie, our whole lives."

"Yes, oh, yes."

Lannie felt a rush of such intense happiness that it almost hurt, but then the curtain shoved aside and a bulky man in an orderly's uniform appeared. "Over to Imaging?"

"Yes, that's me," she said. Everything came flooding back. The baby…the bleeding…not knowing for sure.

She went shaky and sick at once, and Nate knew it. He took her arm and she leaned into his hard body while the orderly fiddled with the gurney, getting it ready to push. "Marry me, Lannie. I want you to say you'll marry me *before* we know if there's still a baby or not, because that's what this is about. I love you no matter what. I love you, the whole package, the whole deal, good and bad, so can you say it, please, can you say yes to me, sweetheart, before we go?"

"Yes. Yes, Nate, I'll marry you."

The orderly began to whistle. "Not to hurry you folks along, or anything." He'd seen it all before.

Lannie and Nate didn't care. He hadn't really seen it all before, because the whole world had sprung up new, just in the last few minutes. What kind of a new world it was going to be, they didn't yet know, but whatever kind it was, whether it was made of happiness or loss, they would discover it together.

Chapter Twenty-Two

"Okay, here comes the picture now."

The ultrasound probe moved across Lannie's stomach, cool and slippery with gel. The ultrasound room was darkened, and the monitor screen still grainy. She and Nate were both focused on it intently, not sure what they would see. He held her hand, his touch so familiar, so wanted always. Her heart had begun to beat faster, and the world had shrunk to just this room.

"Do you remember, the first ultrasound?" he said softly.

"As if I'd ever forget!" She had tears in her eyes, remembering.

There was a baby in there.

They'd seen it, curled and tiny, only recognizing it as human out of sheer faith, it had been so small. But it was moving, and it had a heartbeat, and the bleeding had only been a placental tear. She'd spent two weeks on bed rest just to be safe, but there'd been no more problems after that.

Now, four months later, with winter snow already on the ground, no one could be in any doubt that there was a baby in there. Lannie's stomach bulged hard and round, and the baby kicked Nate in the back at night, when she lay curled against him.

And she loved to lie curled against him, in her lodge at Sheridan Lakes. Construction on their log home overlooking Musk Lake wouldn't start until the spring, by which time their baby would already be born. They hoped to be moved in by their first wedding anniversary in early October, when the leaves would be blazing with orange and yellow and red, the color as spectacular as it had been on their wedding day.

A small wedding, by the way, with a sunny outdoor ceremony on Nate's piece of land, and a quiet dinner in a screened-off section of their own Lavande Restaurant, overlooking the lake. Mom and Dad hadn't thought it appropriate for the Sheridan hotel heiress to have a lavish wedding when she had a baby due next spring, so it hadn't been difficult to organize the event quickly.

And Nate had been right. What you *do* and what you *want*... Those things tell you who you are. Lannie was a person who'd been completely thrilled not to have an enormous wedding.

They'd honeymooned in Hawaii, which was gorgeous for sightseeing in October, and if Lannie's parents were still not one hundred percent approving of her choice, that figure was climbing daily, and had reached, oh, around eighty-eight.

"Here's the head," their obstetrician said. "Already down, which is great. Spine coming around here, backside here... Okay, now we're getting some movement. Ah...what's this? Did you want to know the sex?"

"Yes," said Nate firmly, as ever a man who liked to know what he was dealing with. "Uh...is there definitely a 'this'?"

"There sure is! Look, I'm sure you can see it. Congratulations! You're having a boy."

"A boy!" Lannie whispered. "Wow!"

"Were you wanting a boy?" the obstetrician asked. A middle-aged father of four himself, he had a smile in his voice as he spoke.

"We want whatever comes," Nate answered for them both. "It'll be new, whatever it is, whoever *he* is, he'll be a whole new world for us to discover together."

He'd put into words exactly what Lannie had thought four months ago, as they went for that first ultrasound. Now there was a new world once again. The whole new world of a baby boy, and the best man she could imagine to be his father.

Wow. Just wow.

Lannie couldn't stop smiling.

* * * * *

Silhouette®

COMING NEXT MONTH

Available August 31, 2010

#2065 FROM DOCTOR...TO DADDY
Karen Rose Smith
Montana Mavericks: Thunder Canyon Cowboys

#2066 ONCE A FATHER
Kathleen Eagle

#2067 THE SURGEON'S FAVORITE NURSE
Teresa Southwick
Men of Mercy Medical

#2068 THE COWBOY'S CONVENIENT BRIDE
Wendy Warren
Home Sweet Honeyford

#2069 PROGNOSIS: ROMANCE
Gina Wilkins
Doctors in Training

#2070 IT STARTED WITH A HOUSE...
Helen R. Myers

SPECIAL EDITION

REQUEST YOUR FREE BOOKS!

2 FREE NOVELS PLUS 2 FREE GIFTS!

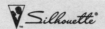

SPECIAL EDITION
Life, Love and Family!

YES! Please send me 2 FREE Silhouette® Special Edition® novels and my 2 FREE gifts (gifts are worth about $10). After receiving them, if I don't wish to receive any more books, I can return the shipping statement marked "cancel." If I don't cancel, I will receive 6 brand-new novels every month and be billed just $4.24 per book in the U.S. or $4.99 per book in Canada. That's a saving of 15% off the cover price! It's quite a bargain! Shipping and handling is just 50¢ per book.* I understand that accepting the 2 free books and gifts places me under no obligation to buy anything. I can always return a shipment and cancel at any time. Even if I never buy another book from Silhouette, the two free books and gifts are mine to keep forever.

235/335 SDN E5RG

Name _____ (PLEASE PRINT) _____

Address _____ Apt. #

City _____ State/Prov. _____ Zip/Postal Code

Signature (if under 18, a parent or guardian must sign)

Mail to the Silhouette Reader Service:
IN U.S.A.: P.O. Box 1867, Buffalo, NY 14240-1867
IN CANADA: P.O. Box 609, Fort Erie, Ontario L2A 5X3

Not valid for current subscribers to Silhouette Special Edition books.

Want to try two free books from another line?
Call 1-800-873-8635 or visit www.morefreebooks.com.

* Terms and prices subject to change without notice. Prices do not include applicable taxes. N.Y. residents add applicable sales tax. Canadian residents will be charged applicable provincial taxes and GST. Offer not valid in Quebec. This offer is limited to one order per household. All orders subject to approval. Credit or debit balances in a customer's account(s) may be offset by any other outstanding balance owed by or to the customer. Please allow 4 to 6 weeks for delivery. Offer available while quantities last.

Your Privacy: Silhouette is committed to protecting your privacy. Our Privacy Policy is available online at www.eHarlequin.com or upon request from the Reader Service. From time to time we make our lists of customers available to reputable third parties who may have a product or service of interest to you. If you would prefer we not share your name and address, please check here. ☐

Help us get it right—We strive for accurate, respectful and relevant communications. To clarify or modify your communication preferences, visit us at www.ReaderService.com/consumerschoice.

SSE10R

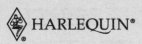

HARLEQUIN®

American ★ Romance®

TANYA MICHAELS
Texas Baby

Instant parenthood is turning Addie Caine's life
upside down. Caring for her young nephew and
infant niece is rewarding—but exhausting! So when
a gorgeous man named Giff Baker starts a short-term
assignment at her office, Addie knows there's no time
for romance. Yet Giff seems to be in hot pursuit....
Is this part of his job, or can he really be falling
for her? And her chaotic, ready-made family!

**Available September 2010
wherever books are sold.**

"LOVE, HOME & HAPPINESS"

www.eHarlequin.com

HAR75325

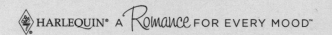
HARLEQUIN® A *Romance* FOR EVERY MOOD™

HARLEQUIN
RECOMMENDED READS
PROGRAM

LOOKING FOR A NEW READ?
**Pick up Michelle Willingham's latest
Harlequin® Historical book**

SURRENDER TO
AN IRISH WARRIOR

Available in September

Here's what readers have to say about this
Harlequin® Historical fan-favorite author

"[T]his book kept me up late into the night…I just had
to find out what happened…I am soooo looking forward
to the next two books Willingham has out."
**—eHarlequin Community Member *Tammys*
on *Her Irish Warrior***

"This was a wonderful story with great characters
and constant twists and turns in the plot that
kept me turning the pages."
**—eHarlequin Community Member *Sandra Hyatt*
on *The Warrior's Touch***

AVAILABLE WHEREVER BOOKS ARE SOLD

HHRECO0910